A DARK DRABBLES ANTHOLOGY

Compiled & edited by
Minions of the Hell Hare

Also available from Black Hare Press

DARK DRABBLE ANTHOLOGIES

WORLDS
ANGELS
MONSTERS
BEYOND
UNRAVEL
APOCALYPSE
LOVE
HATE
OCEANS
ANCIENTS
666

Twitter: @BlackHarePress
Facebook: BlackHarePress
Website: www.BlackHarePress.com

Table of Contents

Foreword

We all have a fascination for things that scare us—the thrill, the heart-stopping jump scares, the terrifying suspense. From the youngest age, we're fascinated by the fiendish and furry, the creepiest critters, the naughty and the nasty. Horror is all around us, from the clowns who hide under our bed, to the things we might drag up from the brook at the bottom of the garden, and the zombies who crawl our streets.

As Megan Feehley, author of our closing drabble, so eloquently says; there is beauty just before the terror…a silken breath taken before the spill of righteousness…the warmth of a licking flame preceding the scald.

So, close the drapes, check the locks, turn on all the lights and get comfortable. But *don't* close your eyes…

Never close your eyes.

Love & kisses, Black Hare Press

Light Sleeper
by Jason Hardy

The third time Cal came back, Tilda found him at the kitchen table. The mongrel stench of deep earth and rot nearly made her retch.

He pushed a knife towards her, handle first. "Please, try again." Beetles flitted about his blackened wounds; he seemed not to notice.

She sat, sighing, and pushed the blade away. "There's gasoline. We could try fire." *Ash and bone. You couldn't come back that way, could you?*

He looked at her with waxen eyes and nodded. "Whatever it takes. I'm just so tired, Tilly."

"I know." Tilda took her late husband's hand. *So am I.*

A Pair of Socks
by Scott G. Gibson

The socks hung alone on the clothesline, swaying stiffly in the afternoon breeze. They were damp from the drizzle of rain earlier in the day, but the fierce sun had dried them again.

Below, the grass reached up, unmown and untidy. Within the jungle of grass, a human body lay, bloated and peeling, its foetid stench unnoticed by any living thing.

The corpse's mouth opened, emitting a long guttural moan, joined by the hungry horde beyond the wooden fence. The zombie stood up, its head dragging the lifeless sock to the ground, before limping off in search of fresh meat.

An Eye for an Eye
by Chris Hewitt

"An eye for an eye," said the optician, scalpel hovering over my unblinking, unmoving pupil. "That's the deal, right?"

My lips tremble, fingers grasp the table to stop my shaking. "I... I'm sorry, I—"

"Was drunk? Yes, I know. I read the police report," he sobs, inching the blade closer. "Sorry, doesn't bring her back though, does it?"

"Please...how is this fair?"

"Fair! Fair would be that I took *your* child from you. But I can't, so this will have to do."

With a flick of his wrist, he slits my pupil's throat.

The other students scream and run.

Parting Lovers
by Emery Blake

Your sensuous lips, so soft under my thumb's caress. Your silky cheek so pale, so tender. Your open eyes, a defiant suffrage against nature's leave. But I can see in them that your heart has already left.

Your touch still haunts me, both in my dreams and when I'm awake. But I have to let you go—it's what you want.

The parting pain is sharp. I feel it; a dull, heavy ache in my heart. Do you feel it, my darling?

I sigh, press one final kiss to your cold lips, close the coffin lid and leave the room.

Widower's Wife
by Kendal Tomson

The faintest brush of your fingertips over my cold, rigid cheek brings my awareness crashing back. As the cloudiness clears from my eyes, the tears on your face leave me gutted.

My dearest love, I swore never to leave you. Don't you see? I never meant to leave. This isn't how our story is supposed to end.

Your lips press against mine and I feel the torrent of your grief sweep through me.

The door closes behind you.

It's not as bad as it looks, darling—you don't see the single tear slip from my eye—*I'll be home soon.*

Munch
by Dire Bonnington

As apocalypses go, this one ain't too bad.

I mean…there's no Macey's, no Pret a Manger. No electricity, no internet, nothing.

But, I'm alive.

And I still have my special edition iPhone MMXXX. I keep it hooked up to my solar charger, keep the battery juices filled up. Always ready.

I still take pictures of my dinner. I've got hundreds of photos ready for when Facebook is back online.

I'm lining up a shot now; I get the angle right, shade the lens from the sun, shoot the girl as she runs.

Then raise my gun and shoot again.

Slippery When Wet
by Teresita E. Dziadura

Daniel worked the night shift. He liked it that way. No people.

Soapy water sloshed as he mopped the hallway floor. Daniel hummed and bopped to the Louisiana blues that thrummed through his earbuds.

He didn't see the shadow. Never heard the low hissing noise as it slithered towards him. An icy tendril wrapped around his throat.

Freezing. Burning.

He screamed into the silence. Blood spattered as smoky talons bit into flesh.

Tearing. Rending.

He fell to the floor, watching his life blood pool by his head. A sign lay crooked in the growing crimson puddle: CAUTION - Slippery When Wet.

Fun Memories
by Benjamin Kurt Unsworth

The lights flicker violently as I think back. I really led a full life. I knew many people as well, but never each for very long. I was a traveller, you see, hopping from place to place. My first was little Bella, then second came Lucille, but don't tell her mother—it'd shatter her heart. Third was Lilly, and she was my favourite. On Holly, I tried something new, and used a knife instead. Then fifth—

My time's up. My cheekbones arch in glee and with a ghoulish grin on my face, the electricity sizzles through my body. I laugh.

Chastity
by Dorann Brooke

Urgent knocking woke Jaycee. She opened her eyes into the subdued light of the hotel room.

Dan, her husband—the surgeon—watched over her.

"Police! Open up!" More insistent banging.

She remembered the tangle of sheets, her yoga instructor, Dan's angry face.

A heart monitor blipped next to her. "What have you done?" she breathed, terrified.

"You know I don't share." His smile didn't touch his eyes.

The door exploded. Officers spilled into the room but faltered at the sight.

"A hemicorporectomy." Dan sneered. "I amputated your body below the waist."

Jaycee made a choking sound.

"No more screwing around."

Final Release
by Meera Dandekar

Billy lived in his old house. His life was taken away by his own mother in an attempt to eliminate all evil from the house.

She had killed herself right then. After all, he was her blood.

But something didn't feel right. Billy felt more alive. His love for his mother did not let him leave the house.

It had been over twenty years. He was stuck inside. There was only one way. He peeled the skin off her body with his fingernails. The blood was dried out, but he didn't mind when he put it on.

He became her.

Home Improvement
by Eddie D. Moore

Yes, I knew about the murders. The basement floor was blood-stained, and dozens of symbols were painted on the walls. My skin crawled just looking at them, but for the price, I couldn't pass it up. I knew that I'd make a killing flipping it.

It took three coats of paint to cover the graffiti, and it was after midnight when I finished. While I was putting the lid on the paint, the lights went out. Cold fingers slowly wrapped around my throat, and my feet refused to move.

A malevolent voice growled, "Fool, those symbols were your only protection."

Midday
by Danielle Bonnin

Paul stood waiting in the icy, cold darkness. His teeth chattered and he hadn't been able to feel his fingers in hours. Even though he was crammed in with hundreds of other people, none of them seemed to give off any heat. A small child looked up at him from under frosted eyelashes. "I'm scared," she whispered, hoarsely.

Suddenly, bright, piercing light filled their world and all heads turned to squint up at the artificial sun.

Uhrn of the planet Dagon, his food processing organ growling loudly, opened the fridge and peered in at his lunch with one large eye.

Cramps
by Catherine Kenwell

The abdominal cramps were debilitating. I folded myself onto the toilet seat. I'd suffered an irritated bowel for as long as I could recall, but never felt pain like this.

I had barely crouched down when a torrent of foul excrement exploded from my hole. Instant relief. Grasping paper to wipe, I felt something wriggle. Peering between my buttocks, I discovered a string-like protuberance dangling towards the fetid bowl. Horrified, my first reaction was to grab it between paper-shrouded fingertips and pull. My insides churned; I let go, and it snapped back up like a frog's tongue catching a fly.

Raróg's Revenge
by Drew Man

Doroteya scooped the cracking egg onto a cloth. Hate-filled eyes squinted at her husband through the window. She marvelled that he always saved the tenderest of caresses for the seedlings but the harshest knocks for her. Her hand went to the small of her back where she knew a mottled bruise blossomed.

Nine days and nights she'd stood sentinel over the incubating egg and now the tiny fire demon was hatching.

She whispered her tears to it.

It launched and flew out the window, soon returning bloodied and exhausted.

Her husband's gory, broken body now food for his precious plants.

Plastic
by Ronnie Smart

Driving back from childcare, the plastic in my water bottle began whispering predictions, telling me its comrades were taking over. Becky sang "Moana" in the backseat, oblivious.

At home, I discovered my television was encased in Bubble Wrap. Cling film had left the drawer, covering all the fruit. I turned; a plastic sheet was transparently gripping Becky's head. I clawed the plastic into the bin.

When I look outside, plastic bags float through the air like flying jellyfish. They fly past cars whispering dread thoughts. Sometimes, swimming at the beach, I feel their plastic tendrils. They pull at my feet.

Mrs Orton's Porch Step
by Danyel Bardo

I leave the pub, yell a drunken, "Goodbye," and head home.

From Mrs Orton's porch, a pumpkin still mouths its flame-coloured scream. The beer-filled me decides I want it. I sneak in the gate, giggling like a child—can't wait to show the guys my prize.

As my hands reach out, the door opens. Mrs Orton stands there in her nightdress, toothless gummy smile wrinkling her face. "Tut-tut," she sneers. With a flick of her wrist, my world fades to black.

* * *

A year goes by before I see my friends. I scream from Mrs Orton's porch, but they don't notice.

Bludgeon
by Grace R. Reynolds

Stephen slammed his left palm down onto the grain of the workbench in his shop and inhaled deeply. With the smoothed wooden grip of his chisel, he drove the tool deep into his index finger to separate the digits. Though the blow was backed with immense strength, Stephen had not quite severed the joint, and now the steel core of the instrument, wedged partially into the bloodied appendage, had fallen out of its socket. He gritted his teeth and began to hammer the handle against the metal until, finally, he had bludgeoned the plummy finger into a perfectly ruined stump.

Nine Ladies Dancing
by Danelley Beat

She dances for him: *en pointe*, lightly skimming the dark wood of the tabletop.

"Enchanting, Number Eight," he whispers huskily. He watches from the shadows, hooded eyes black as a starless night, dark hair falling across his face.

Assemblé...changement...petit battement. A final jerky *chaînés*, then she is still. Eyes closed, she awaits his critique.

"Beautiful, Mon Cher," he breathes, awestruck.

"Nine, how will you compete with such a magnificent performance?" he asks of the next girl.

Nine moans through the gag. Her watering eyes plead as he pulls the rope, and the noose tightens.

En pointe, she dances.

A Father's Love
by Reuben Paul

The music played, soft and romantic, throughout the burrow and they danced slowly to the tune.

With her head on his shoulder, and her ears draped down his back, he led the sway, recalling how he'd wooed her back in their younger days, before all the responsibility that family brought. How they'd frolicked in the fields chasing butterflies and enjoying the morning sun.

Their beautiful leverets, the spoils of their love, bounced excitedly around them and he smiled, lips curling to reveal white fangs.

He'd forever mourn her death, but at least the babies would have a hearty meal tonight.

Blood
by Brian Maycock

My thoughts race.

Carried away by swelling voices, faces, people appearing from everywhere.

It started so well, everyone was saying. There was a spirit that real change was happening. Here. Now.

But then the first bottle was thrown. The first arrest made.

I do not blame either side. I was with no one but myself.

I came to feed.

The chaos gave me perfect cover. A young man, stumbling ahead. I leant, piercing his skin.

Sweeter than any kiss.

Then—flames spitting from burning cars, shop windows gaping dumbly through jagged openings while looters tumbled in—I slip away.

Sated.

Musings from the Circles of Hell
by Matt Krizan

The screaming of the damned still gets to me. With all the atrocities I've seen over the millennia, you'd think I'd be numb to them by now. I can gaze upon demons rending living flesh and devouring livers, and spleens, and still-beating hearts without even batting an eye. The sight of railroad spikes being driven through wrists and ankles as sinners are crucified moves me not at all. The endless rows of serried spears with men, women, and children impaled upon them fade into the background like wallpaper.

And yet, after all this time, the screams still turn me on.

The Host
by Matthew Stevens

I woke to find my arms covered with dozens of tiny red bumps. They looked like mosquito bites and itched. So, I scratched until a couple swelled. One popped, expelling a small grey cloud.

It led to a dry cough. An incessant tickle in my throat. Followed by intense stomach pain.

Had to be a bug of some kind.

I wasn't wrong. Entirely.

When the pain woke me overnight, it was too late. My insides wanted to be outside.

Doubled over the toilet, in the dark, the click of giant mandibles echoed up the stairs.

She had come to harvest.

Quiet
by Michelle Brooks

Sandra screamed at the crying doll, "Shut up!"

What a horrible prank to be playing on her, only weeks after losing her daughter at birth!

Who was controlling the toy, causing it to shriek non-stop?

She'd solve that mystery, eventually. First, Sandra had to silence the noisy brat...

Soon, her husband, Hugh, returned home with groceries. He found Sandra upstairs, scissors clenched in her fist.

She beamed. "I removed its voice box!"

Their son, Owen, the surviving twin, lay motionless in his crib.

Yes, Sandra had been suffering. But Hugh never imagined she'd fall victim to a postpartum psychotic break.

Wildflowers
by Matthew M. Montelione

Jenna stirred on a bed of wildflowers. She opened her eyes, breathing in the summer scent. *What a nice nap.* She sat up, stretching her arms. The sunlight bathed the lush forest near her family's farmhouse in deep yellow. She was at peace; away from the noisy city where she lived and worked.

The wildflowers stirred suddenly beneath her. She heard cryptic voices in the wind, speaking in strange tongues. Before she could react, she was ensnared in tangled roots. She screamed as they twisted around her legs, dragging her underground.

She felt blood leaving her body, enriching the wildflowers.

Whore Paint
by Payton Riley

"Don't. Move." Shana paused, lip brush in hand. "If you keep wriggling, your lipstick is going to smudge, and I'll have to start over. Do you want that?"

In the chair, Halle stilled, her eyes wide with terror.

"Bad enough your mascara is already running. I *told* you to hold *still!*"

A quick slap to her trembling wrist made Halle cry out.

"Now you've gone and pulled a stitch." Shana grabbed a scissor, roughly severing each stitch holding the girl's lips closed, sharply yanking each thread through.

Dabbing away the oozing blood, Shana picked up the needle. "Now. *Hold. Still.*"

Bug Translator
by P.R. Tough

He had finally done it.

The robotic voice in his earpiece said, "Find food. Find food. Find food," repeatedly.

He released the trigger on his latest invention and could not stop smiling. The bug translator worked! The ant was out looking for food.

Eugene pointed the gun at a honeybee. "Find nectar. Find nectar. Find nectar."

Still smiling, Eugene remembered he had seen a centipede in the bathtub earlier. He almost ran to the bathroom to find out what the centipede was saying. "Mother is waiting for you, human." Eugene smashed his invention on the centipede and never smiled again.

I'll Come Back for Justice
by Russell Hemmell

The cat was cursed—they knew it at once.

Evil. They should've never rescued her.

Black as the darkest night, a ghost-like meow, fierce gaze. And how did she know the ranch so well?

They ignored the Indian mass graves festering in the backyard, where forgotten victims of old slaughtering lay furious and unavenged.

One night, the cat crept upstairs, her paws pushing the bedchamber's door until it cracked open.

Blood. Body parts scattered around. Slaughter in plain sight—a raptus of madness engulfing the household.

Justice was done. Until next time.

Purring, green eyes like flames, she slipped away.

We Came to Him
by Gary Rubidge

We didn't know from where he came, or when. He was just *here*. His teachings drew people in like moths to a flame, captivating and hypnotising us with his fervour, consuming everyone with his plans.

Our judgement became clouded as we took up arms against our neighbours, suspecting everyone not of our likeness to be the enemy in need of annihilation.

Everyone eagerly flocked to the cause; our loyalty rewarded with the ultimate honour of sitting by his side for eternity, gifted with riches beyond our wildest dreams.

And we knew him by the rudimentary birthmark on his head: 666

Congeries
by D.J. Tyrer

The sign above the tent says 'Congeries'. Sounds exotic—hicks who can't resist the lure of the strange pay a dime to tramp inside.

Within, a vat, and in it something bubbles—a congeries of blisters, oozing, throbbing. Occasionally, an eye, oddly human, blinks over the rim and boneless limbs reach out, flailing.

Spectators jump back, laughing, shrieking, delighted.

Then, when night falls, that congeries of throbbing globes flops out of the vat and crawls through the shadows of the carnival and into the nearby town in search of flesh to absorb.

A child vanishes to a cry of "Tekeli-li!"

The Midnight Circus
by Sheldon Woodbury

A shadowy caravan snaked its way down dark country roads, with its mysteries and horrors shrouded from view until it was time to rumble to a stop and hoist its tattered old tents that fluttered like moonlit ghosts in the night. A whispery call was unleashed that could only be heard in the slumbering darkness of children's dreams, followed soon after by the sleepy padding of their stumbling feet. At the last possible moment before daybreak, the ancient circus rolled off again, sneaking away without any sound at all, except for the horrific blare of mothers and fathers howling screams.

A Cell of Flesh
by Micah Castle

A home, a body, a prison. Is there a difference? A cell keeping things in. Hallways, doorways, stairs; ventricles, arteries, veins. Pushing against walls of sinew and muscle, clawing at the fibres containing what pleads for release.

What I truly am; what words and fists kept within; what bruises and crying only rooted deeper; what incessant, berating thoughts droned in an unravelling mind so desperate to understand why it was *wrong*.

A guided blade peels flesh away like ribbon, blood spills in rivulets, and soon what I have always *meant* to become emerges from what I was forced to be.

Nothing is for Nothing
by Angie Wallace

No one is home.

A blood moon shines into a study littered with curious artefacts. Moonlight throws the intruder's shadow over an open book, grand and ancient. Found at last!

The exposed illustration entices her as it distorts and moves with coruscating blue, crimson and gold. The shifting image compels her to get closer; to touch it, to feel it.

Too late, she tries to remove her hand. Swirling colours cover her arm and body. She screams.

The grimoire absorbs her skin as it dissolves.

Soon there is a new illustration.

Another flayed seeker added to the *Book of Souls*.

The Lady in the Ground
by Jodie Francis

I wasn't supposed to hear that—I could see it in Daddy's eyes.

Why are they so dark? I don't remember them being so dark.

His head started twitching, like our puppy, Timmy, does when he's excited. But Daddy wasn't excited. He was very angry. At me. Mummy started whispering in his ear, and then shooed me out of the room like when Timmy's been naughty.

So what if he had put a lady in the ground? He could always pull her out again.

"She's your daughter, you can't!"

"Get off me, Sheila!"

"Daddy, why are you holding a knife?"

Not Welcome
by Andrew Davis

These illegals are not welcome here.

Peter Jacobson smiled happily to himself as he finished his latest column. It was definitely going to outrage the armchair socialists. Stretching, he started to mull over his next piece. He could even start now.

His hands seized up. Yelping in shock, he watched in horror as, one by one, his nails peeled back and dropped to the carpet. The skin around his fingers slowly unwound, twisting agonisingly backwards.

His flayed body was found in News Corp's office the next morning. Carefully arranged next to him, his skin spelled three words: *NOT WELCOME HERE*.

All Our Trespasses
by Ali House

As she drew closer, he noticed the thick red blood coating her mouth and chin. In one hand was a sharpened blade that had recently performed terrible, unspeakable deeds.

"You have trespassed and witnessed our most secret ritual," she growled.

The hooded figures restraining him tightened their grip.

"There is only one remedy."

He froze as she put the blade to his throat, tracing his jugular vein.

Suddenly, she pulled the blade away, slicing open her palm. She held her hand out to him.

"Join us."

He stared at the blood dripping from the wound, then began to drink hungrily.

Hunger Be Damned
by Michael D. Evans

I exist only in darkness. I feel the crushing weight of the world around me, kept at bay by these four walls. The stale air filled with a damp, earthy aroma seems so distant. None of these things matter, only the hunger matters.

Hunger like rage. Hunger like nitrogen, burning me inside out. Hunger like electricity, jolting and contorting my body. Hunger wipes my thoughts from me. Hunger calls me back from the beyond.

To hell with that, I was promised rest. *Rest in peace.* Let the others devour the world—I am staying in my grave.

Hunger be damned.

Why am I
Under Your Spell?
by Matt Hawkers

The tilt of your smile is mesmerising, and the soft curve of your cupid's bow sublime. But it isn't that.

Your eyes sparkle and hypnotise; I've seen men walk into lampposts, distracted by those shimmering ebon pools. But, still, it isn't that.

The slope of your shoulders, the rise of your breasts, the sway of your hips as you walk—all quite heavenly.

But, no; it's the moist trail your tongue leaves across your lips, the hunger in your eyes, the sigh on your lips as your teeth sink in.

Now I'm yours forever, but you had me at, "Hello."

Long Pig Tartare
by Peter Kerby

"What the fuck are you doing?" Freddy asked. His vocal cords still worked but his Zee speech grunts caused spittle to fly everywhere.

"I'm hungry." I grunted. Freddy had become annoying recently, and I was getting sick of his negativity. Besides, we hadn't eaten in days, and beggars couldn't be choosers—Freddy knew the rules.

"But, April—"

I stopped gnawing the leg, narrowed my eyes at him and spat venomously, "What?"

"It's raw!" he exclaimed. "Look at it!"

I stopped eating and we both turned slowly to look at the still-quivering *Sujihiki* embedded in Gary's left eye.

An Exit Is Not the Same as an Entrance
by Marcelo Medone

The weary man arrives at a dilapidated motel in the middle of nowhere.

"I got lost and it's getting dark. Any vacant rooms?"

The receptionist smiles.

"It seems that you're the only guest. Thank God you came."

Just then, fierce growls come from the neighbouring forest.

"Are there bears around here?"

"No, sir. All bears fled."

The clerk guides him to his room, on the ground floor. There is a barred window that overlooks the forest, next to another door.

"An emergency exit?"

"It's an entrance. He gets hungry at night," says the clerk, who leaves, locking up the door.

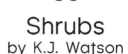

Shrubs
by K.J. Watson

"Ensure you maintain the shrubs around my house," Skrite ordered.

"Shouldn't I grow food for the starving villagers instead, my lord?" Thomas the gardener asked.

"Don't be insolent," Skrite replied.

That evening, Thomas consulted a witch about the shrubs and took her advice.

In the autumn, the aristocracy gathered to dine and cavort at Skrite's Grand Ball. Emaciated villagers gathered to watch.

"Stand back," Thomas advised.

At midnight, the shrubs' roots surged from the soil. Nourished by the blood and bones of those who had succumbed to starvation, the roots dragged Skrite's house, and its screaming occupants, down into oblivion.

Too Expensive
by Trina Jacobs

"We can't afford monsters," said Mommy.

"It's not the output, it's the upkeep," said Daddy.

"But everybody has one."

But something grabbed at Dani's ankles with its wicked claws as she climbed into bed.

Then the neighbour's missing cat showed up. At least its head did. It rolled out from under the bed, all bloody.

Mommy checked the closet. Daddy checked under the bed. Nothing there.

Mommy hugged Dani. Daddy chuckled, then screamed as something dragged him under the bed. Mommy held Dani tight. More screams from under the bed, then crunching and slurping noises.

Monsters were much too expensive.

Fresh Meat
by John Lane

On State Highway 6, Jack discovered, then followed, an unmarked dirt road. Mumbled voices called his name.

On the other side stood Witch's Butcher Shop. Something unseen pulled him inside, past the "Fresh Meat" sign.

Jack noticed nothing but empty coolers. The unseen chorus spoke, "Tired."

He tried to block them out, but they continued. "Tired. TIRED."

Jack's brain was crushed. His body collapsed on the wooden floor.

A one-eyed, hairy woman with a chainsaw emerged. The power tool cut through Jack's torso like butter.

The rest of her coven came through the walls, salivating over the day's "fresh meat."

Silence is Golden
by Rowan Skylar

Crunch!

Crista leaned back against the front door, basking in soundlessness, her countenance beatific. She slipped inside, closed the door with a barely audible *snick!* Tiptoed down the hall; she almost made it. The bundle in her arms squirmed, throwing her off-balance.

Her foot landed hard, squarely on a creaky floorboard. *Bollox.* She froze.

"Crista?"

Silence. "Yeah, Mum." Her mum approached, and she panicked; tossed the bundle into a houseplant.

"You're late."

"Oh." Wide eyes fixated on bleeding leaves. "Sorry."

Mum turned, snatched up the bundle and ripped it open.

Pointing inside with bloody fingers. "Where'd this moggy come from?"

Reflection
by Andra Dill

The boogeyman does not live under beds or in closets. She lives in mirrors and looks exactly like me, except for the crusted flakes of blood that rim her nails and the corners of her smirking mouth. Telling adults about her leads to gentle assurances, then exasperated lectures, doctor visits, and finally, bitter little pills.

Dad shaves while I, eyes downcast, brush my teeth. The tapping startles me into glancing up. Traced in a patch of her fogged breath are the familiar words "let me out." A ragged nail jabs the glass. Terror seizes me as a spidery crack appears.

A Woman Scorned
by Delena Broṭhaigh

Dark clouds sprawled across the sky, and a hot wind billowed in from the thrashing sea as the brassy glare of the coming storm drained colour from the horizon. Sand whipped into angry, whirling clouds around me, and my hair buffeted around my head, stinging my cheeks.

I raised my hands higher, my face contorted with rage, and summoned the children of Aeolus.

A winged, aged man rose up from the churning surf, towering above me—his, a face of thunder—and the burning winds followed, caressing the trees and raising the tides.

By Notus' hand, revenge would be mine.

There Goes 666
by Rajiv de Sega

He came when the day fell silent
and the moon's silver painted rooftops.
Nine cats howled behind their windows
and drew claws down the panes.
A dog cowered in the dirt
on the night the man came.

Alas, here the air grew tepid,
for calculated steps brought glacial chills.
Six virgins, their wrists bound, cried:
There goes devil six, six, six.
A hag among them kicked—screamed:
Here comes my six, six, six.

He freed the sacrificial witches and
fast set them upon the town;
bound the wailing by the neck,
seared and left them for the
birds to peck.

Little Sacrifices
by Mason H. Hilden

Tucker slept soundly in Scott's arms, even through the cultist's chanting. He was so content, so young. Sacrificing Tucker would finalise the summoning of a child of the Great Old Ones.

When it was time, Scott didn't hesitate as he slit Tucker's throat. The puppy thrashed about feebly as its life drained away.

Minutes passed before the summoning occurred. Tucker's body convulsed and exploded inside out through its mouth. What was left was a grotesque hellhound.

The beast growled deep, as it spied Scott, still holding the bloody knife. Being summoned from its plane made it both angry and hungry.

Harvest
by Sabeen Sadiq

Here we are again. Running out of time with all the days in the world gone by already. Still, there's no point in waiting for the product to coagulate. Throw a few more taps in, and ramp up the drain. Suck them dry and jar it, pronto. Sure, we already have more than enough. We'll get it all back in time, after all. But supply-side economics is a beautiful thing. Which means; keep it coming. We done? Got every last drop? Right, let's send these dumb bastards back and see how much the next batch pays for this soul crap.

ZoZo
by Kenna Robins

"You want to know my secret?"

* * *

We were having a laugh, reminiscing amidst boxes in the attic. Until Kaylee held up a spirit board.

After too much wine, and lacking sense, we set to playing.

The planchet moved, giving a string of correct answers. Kaylee freaked, breaking contact—setting the demon free.

It attacked; her blood misted my face.

It grinned at me, still bathed in my sister's blood.

The Hell gate snapped closed behind it.

* * *

They labelled me her murderer, but it's my secret that turned me mad. One I've never shared.

The demon dragged her into Hell—alive.

Emma
by Christine Bottas

We got a call from Emma last night. The line crackled as she spoke.

Her mama and I started weepin'. I thought my heart would explode; it thudded against my ribs like a sledgehammer. Ma had to sit down in the ol' paisley print chair. She fanned herself and said she was faint. I'm sure I went as white as Ma's bleached bed sheets.

Emma said she was comin' home.

But Emma died two years ago.

We buried her in the woods, the crow-filled ones not too far from our farm, after I'd filled our only daughter with bullet holes.

Windows of the Soul
by Joanna Hawkers

"I like your eyes."

Stirring her drink, Meg rolled her emerald greens. "Thanks." Turning away, she immediately dismissed the speaker.

Her eyes sparkled while she laughed, and drank, and danced with her friends into the wee hours. Eventually she stumbled out, headed home.

* * *

Ow, I left my contact lenses in.

Rising from a groggy sleep, Meg blinked awake—or tried to blink. She found herself bound, with her eyes prised open.

Her muffled panic caught her captor's attention. "How unfortunate for you. It'll hurt more awake."

The enucleation spoon glinted in the light. "You really have the most amazing eyes."

Well Done
by Pauline Yates

Death from slipping inside an empty industrial waste bin at the height of summer is a fate I refuse to accept. I can't climb out, so I leave my body to numb the agony of being seared like a steak on a hot plate. The visual assault is as brutal. My feet, my fingers disintegrate. Blisters bubble. Pop. Flesh melts, fodder for the flies. Conceding, I beg Death to open its shears and cut me free. Life responds instead: a shout, a ladder. Lifted from the bin, I'm sucked back into my body, a crueller fate dispensed: recovery in Hell.

Selena the Sorceress
by Fred White

Alone in the darkened auditorium, Aldo sat transfixed as Selena the Sorceress shimmered before him, a holographic projection of startling fidelity. "I hope you're ready for your new reality, lover. I need you desperately!"

The projection solidified into sinuous, aromatic flesh. Selena slid her fingers across his chest and moved slowly…south.

Fully aroused, Aldo ignored the dread welling up from his gut.

She brought her hands to the sides of his head and began massaging. The sensation was intoxicating. But then her hands squeezed tighter, and tighter; his arousal turned into horror until his head burst into Selena's open mouth.

Pepper
by Jennifer Lai

The guard drags his keys along the prison bars, then hands me a bowl with liquid the colour of uncooked rice water. "Dinner."

I stick my finger in and touch something soft and grainy. "What is this?"

"Soup," he cackles.

Something wiggles around my finger. A black dot surfaces. Followed by another. And another. Soon, the bowl is a sea of pepper.

It's been three days since they've fed me. I don't even remember what food tastes like anymore.

But I know it doesn't move.

It's just soup, I tell myself as I slurp the chunky, warm liquid. *Peppered soup*.

Skinny Dipping
by Kevin Singer

Time to drown again.

Allison despised her one-piece. Soon she'd be rid of it. She swam toward the lifeguard's chair and imagined him: tall, lithe, golden skin.

The chair was empty.

Allison almost quit, but then she spied the lone sunbather. She splashed and flailed until hands rescued her. On the sand, she took in his body. Young. Fit. She was very pleased.

It took ten minutes for the drugs to render him unconscious. It took two hours to carve the skin from his frame. After three weeks of curing, Allison slipped on her latest skinsuit. It felt like home.

The Groom Arrives
by Stephen Bustanoby

The mistress moon presses me. Pushes me through the bloody swamp I just created. Bare, transforming, dagger-armed paws slosh through guts, limbs, heads. It's a new night; it starts again. Silver spikes of a full moon twisting my body and mind into an ancient beast.

I'm to be wed!

A white angel appears through trees. Colours, flowers, sparkling lights embrace her. I know her. How? My searing chest rages—she is only meat and blood. What more is there? I tear apart those in my way of the angel. Her throat milky, swollen with blood—

May I kiss the bride?

Bloody Hell
by Louise Zedda-Sampson

Estelle's spare key isn't under the mat. She promised it would be. Rob shoulders the door, crashing in on the third charge, then loses his breakfast on the polished oak. Estelle lays supine on the blood-soaked couch, a skinless sculpture of only muscle and bone. Skin hangs in strips around the room; puddles red, viscous and glistening pool underneath.

Even like this, she's beautiful. Her legs are parted. Ready. He chides himself for the thought.

The door shuts behind him. Footsteps. "Welcome," Satan says. "Join us."

Estelle's skinless face turns—is she *smiling*?

"Yes, Rob. You always wanted a threesome."

Cherished Time
by James S. Austin

"It is with a heavy heart I must say goodbye to you, my love." Deidrick softly spoke as he stood before friends and family at the funeral. "To believe you were taken so swiftly from us."

Images and emotions filled him. Her shocked expression. The warmth of the blood. The tugging on her intestines.

"You gave us life and hope," he continued.

This was his seventh wife in this millennium. Convincing someone to fall in love was a difficult undertaking.

"I will cherish the time you gave."

The ritual was precise and unflinching, but so was extending one's earthly existence.

The Procrastinator
by Ben Thomas

He danced around the pyre. The symbols on his face, etched in white, glowed in the firelight, and the heat warmed his cool skin.

As flames flickered, she screamed, face contorted in pain.

He watched her skirts catch fire, and the blaze quickly engulfed her dress. As hot, orange fingers teased her neck, burning her skin, a wave of satisfaction swept through him.

She glared down at him, melting eyes of hatred boring into him, and said,

"Alright, babe? I've brought you a nice cuppa."

And his mind blinked back to the still-blank Word document in front of him.

The Forest Demon
by Aria Sky

Milo hated working in the Kleczanów Forest. It stirred his hackles with half-remembered tales learned at his Babka's knee, of forest demons and burial grounds.

For two days he'd heard whistling, even gone in search of it yesterday. Coffee in hand, Milo glared as the sawblades of his feller buncher bit deeply into the last sacred Aspen.

A shadow fell. He looked, expecting the old man. Instead, it stood upright; a bear's height; clawed with fangs like a wildcat. A single swipe opened Milo, neck to navel.

All that was left: a stack of blood-soaked timber and spilled coffee cup.

I'm So Close
by Stephen Herczeg

Blood rains down. My latest victim hangs by the ankles above—a long deep gash, showering me in their crimson life source.

This one leaves me six shy. A lifetime of work to achieve my goal. All those years ago, when Lucifer called out to me from the deep void of my mind. Allocating me the task of exemplify the number of the beast in corpses. And now there are only half a dozen left to kill.

Sirens grab my attention. Red and blue lights flash.

No. Not now. Not when I'm so close to completion.

Satan will be furious.

Time to Play
by Sam Stephens

Jenny pulled the blanket up, dreading the footsteps outside her bedroom door. Some nights were mercifully silent, too many were not.

Her breath quickened. First one footstep, then another. Her door creaked. The figure entered.

This would be the last time, she thought. No more.

"It's time to play, baby girl."

"I can't, Daddy."

"Why?"

"Because you're dead."

She squirted the walking corpse with lighter fluid and flicked a match.

She cried as she watched the dead flesh blister and peel. Through the flames and the screams, she whispered, "I'm sorry, Daddy. It's time for you to go to heaven."

The Dog's Dinner
by Petina Strohmer

They were looking. Looking and laughing. Again.

"Saw your mum doing the 'walk of shame' again this morning."

"Mutton dressed as lamb."

"What does the old tart think she looks like? All done up like a dog's dinner."

Marcie walked past the other teenagers in the park and took the dog home, her cheeks aflame.

Her mother laughed at her, as always. "I do what I like," she slurred drunkenly. "You should try it sometime, you miserable bitch!"

Good advice, for once. Marcie looked at the dog as she lifted the meat cleaver above her mother's head. "You hungry, boy?"

Let It End!
by Amanda Cecelia Lang

They stop chewing me as I die. Virus transmitted, they trample onward, decaying, soulless.

The plague works slower than teeth. My thoughts are desperate fingers clawing for the end. Infection boils through me, bringing fevered dreams of heaven, convulsions…blessed darkness.

Am I *finally* dead?

Amid the stillness, chains scrape the pavement.

My eyes open. Soul loosened, I stand, ethereal, healed. Released!

Behind me, my half-eaten body rises too. The shackles that bind us grow taut.

"You're one of us now," says a passing spirit.

I stare, horror-struck, as she's jerked onward by puppet master chains and her everlasting corpse.

Unbroken Bonds
by Nicole Kay

The tidal pool rippled with colour as she harvested the dulse—*Pretty as church glass.*

Piteous chirping drove Mara to untangle leathery kelp from an orphaned otter pup.

She and the pup bonded over the months of nursing. She wept the day she returned him to the water.

* * *

Years later, Mara was hanging washing near the river when she was attacked.

From the water, flew a furred shape—uncanny speed and a flash of sharp teeth. Her attacker fell, a bloody hole through his middle.

The dobhar chú turned, its fur, gore-slicked whiskers dripping blood.

Her pup had come home.

Black Eyes
by Dustin Pinney

He listened at the door.

"Let us in."

"To use your phone."

Two kids, approximately sixteen, without phones?

Through the peephole, he saw a boy and girl, standing just outside of the porch light, faces in shadow.

"Come closer," he said.

"Will you let us in?"

"Depends."

The girl's voice changed. "On what?"

"Step. Forwards."

They did.

Two expressionless faces with obsidian eyes.

He opened the door.

They entered his home.

The ghostly kids smiled, started to speak, then stopped.

Rows of black eyeballs were mounted on his mantle.

Locking the door, he said, "You came to the wrong house."

Hells Bells
by Tom Trussel

The bells of the great tower have fallen silent, years of funding cuts caught up at last. Bribes, intimidation and a computer hack secure the refurbishment contract for the Darkpact Builders Co.

Specialist builders are shipped in to toil around the clock. Often heard but never seen, they work for years behind dark scaffolding.

New Year's Eve. Party time. Thousands gather to hear the famous bell's toll once more. The impatient crowds count down together. Three! Two! One!

DOOM! Discordant knells resound. *DOOM*! Waking the darkness within. *DOOM*! The crowds go wild. *DOOM*! The city burns as the madness spreads.

COVID Sausage
by Mason Santiago

Rose pads from fridge to couch, socks cleaning a path in dirty tiles. She sits, forgets why, rises again, returns to the fridge to stare blankly at bulging milk bottles, moulding salad.

* * *

Joshua, sick but hungry, takes a risk. Silently, he descends the stairs, alert, rheumy eyes on the exit. He makes a run for the door.

He's slow, sneezes.

Ahchoo!

And she's fast.

Too weak, he succumbs to his fate.

She feeds—fetid breath and decaying flesh against his skin—finally satiated.

* * *

Rose pads from couch to fridge, opens the door, stares in at moulding salad and COVID sausage.

Hope
by Kelly Matsuura

Days have passed. I'm still strapped to the table, but I'm alive. There's hope.

The scent of raw meat causes me to turn my head. My captor is scraping flesh from a deer carcass with a butcher's knife. Blood drips down from the creature's shiny skeletal hand, to wrist, to its elbow.

No flesh, only bones. A walking, talking skeleton.

It sees me watching and pauses.

"If you eat animals, why am I here?" I ask.

It swaps its knife for a hand mirror and holds it up. "I did you yesterday."

My head is now a bare skull too.

The Dabbler
by Marie Dean

Jess had always been a good person—sweet, kind-hearted, gentle, pure—until she decided to dabble in the occult.

And the occult dabbled back.

* * *

A screech like nails on a chalkboard filled the room, piercing eardrums.

Half the "coven" bolted. The other half stood rooted in terror. No one had believed it would *work*.

The demon laughed and disappeared.

Except, it hadn't. The demon was inside now, a constant torment—whispering, urging, painstakingly corrupting. Jess resisted, cried, and pleaded…uselessly.

You! Get out of my head! Please leave, please!

The demon just laughed, lifting Jess' bloody hand for the final blow.

Wicked Offerings
by Delaney McCormick

Mardochée watched from the shadows of overgrown cypress trees as the old woman circled thrice around a sun-bleached tomb. Mambo Josetté was the most feared Voodoo priestess in the Bayou; her power eclipsed only by her greed.

Rage overtook the man as he leapt from the shadows, sinking his blade deep between the wicked woman's ribs. Josetté's pained howl was quickly silenced as blood splattered against the crumbling tomb.

"That's for Esmalée," Mardochée growled as he carved her still-beating heart from her chest. Dropping it alongside the other offerings at the tomb, Mardochée licked the blade as he walked away.

Shopkeep
by Rachel Reeves

Please, please, have a sit, have a sit! It is simply dreadful out there, just dreadful. What luck that you stumbled into my shop! I'm not normally open today, day of rest and all that, but I had, well, let's call it a feeling. Feelings are amazing, aren't they? There are so many of them. Fear, arousal, jealousy, sadness, ennui, every one a dish best savoured. Come here, browse my wares, you poor lost soul. I won't bite…much. Everyone has a price, and I pride myself in getting the best deals for my customers. What can I get you?

Wendigo Winds
by Mercy Marie

The winter storms had come early. They wrapped the world in blinding white. Day followed night followed day until it was only darkness and skirling winds.

She'd heard her husband's cry from the tree line and ran towards his voice. But it wasn't his voice, just the chittering of a gaunt-limbed shadow's sharp teeth.

The Wendigo sat hunched over, staring into what remained of the previous night's fire.

She looked over her shoulder at what remained of her husband. Tears left icy tracks through the bloody smears around her lips.

The voice in the wind still hungered.

She still hungered.

Getting to Know You
by Nick Petrou

I peel one layer of you at a time. You're pinker by the day. Your cries grow louder. But you've run out of tears. You said I didn't know you. You didn't let me try. Your cheekbones sit higher. Your eyes are glass. Your family won't find you. And what do you need them for anyway? I know you better than anyone, now. I'm working to the marrow of you. When your muscles fall from your bones like rope, what will I find? What does it matter? Getting to know someone is my favourite part. One layer at a time.

Loch Fest
by Soren Ringh

Jacob frowned at the loud buzzing in his head. It was giving him a headache.

Something moved along the loch's surface.

"Jacob!" his mother called from the trail. The wall of conifers hiding him from her nagging eyes. Eighteen, and she still treated him like a child.

"Coming!"

The buzzing stopped. She was there, in his head, before he actually saw her. A woman, treading the deeper water offshore. Jacob felt the need to join her.

Paddling out, Jacob saw little ones schooling about. One grabs his leg.

My, what sharp teeth they have!

Ha! Just like in the fairy—

Atrophy
by Beth W. Patterson

I just wanted a trophy.

Nobody had ever picked me to play sports. But I discovered that if you bury the team captain up to his neck and give him enough food and water to survive, his body stops growing.

All I had to do was feign a summer job at the park with my wheelbarrow and shovel, zealously pretending to guard my bottle of Gatorade. That jock couldn't resist knocking me down and guzzling my drink in front of me. The drug tackled him instantly.

By the time the authorities dug him out, he looked like a collectable figurine.

Devil's Deal
by Jade Cinders

He is here. My bones reverberate with the echo of his hooved feet on the tile. He stops before me, penetrating me with his crimson glare.

"I've brought payment," I say.

I step aside, revealing the bound child trembling behind me.

"A life for a life?" he asks.

I think of my sick wife and nod.

"Deal."

Smiling, he shoots a clawed hand into my gut. I feel a rip inside, then see it—my heart, still beating—in his hand. He takes a bite out of it, like a boy with an apple, as I collapse into eternal darkness.

Groundhog Day
by Dasie Barkus

"How are you today, Anne?" Dr Gardener, the lead psychiatrist, asked.

"You cannot win, warlock," Anne spat, grasping at her hospital gown.

"Doctor Gardener is not a witch," Dr Jones interjected. "You're having a schizophrenic hallucination."

"Unenlightened fool," Anne sneered.

She saw Dr Gardener smirk, and anger began to pulse through her body. Her eyes glowed and, suddenly, Dr Jones combusted into a fiery mass, his melting face screaming soundlessly.

"Naughty." Dr Gardener laughed. "But I will wear you down, witch. I'm winning."

With a flick of the warlock's hand, Dr Jones returned to his pre-spell state, none the wiser.

Remodel
by Michael Gregory

Winston screamed and squirmed as his ear was severed and staple-gunned to his cheek.

His attacker laughed. "Should be easier now to hear your own lies."

Winston had been hired to flip the Courtland House, the site of decades-old family murders.

The building: eerie. The pay: great. Well worth the shivers.

Until killer Caleb Courtland escaped prison, returned home.

Until the psychopath caught Winston at work, sawed off the contractor's feet, and used nails to secure laminate flooring to Winston's shins.

"Changing *you* for the better," Caleb insisted.

He slit open Winston's belly, eager to replace innards with copper piping.

The Ten Year Itch
by Victor J. Amadeous Beowulf IV

There was an incessant itch in Teddy's ear—it needed scratching.

His finger wasn't long enough.

"This goddamn eczema!"

He was sitting underneath a pecan tree in an oversized burgundy camping chair with his wife, Kari.

Her face was like the moon, layers of makeup coating craters along its surface. Porcelain cracks along her cheeks.

"This itch!" he said, standing, his oversized ass lifting the chair from the ground. He freed himself after a brief struggle, bent down, and grabbed a long stick.

"Scratch my ear with this, Kari."

"What?"

"Like this," Teddy said, ramming the stick through Kari's ear.

Gorge
by John West

Trapped in a mountain gorge. So much for Mother's cheap rope.

Barry could starve. He'd seen those movies.

He checked his supplies. Gas stove. Matches. But no food. The fall had ripped a hole in that side of the bag.

He also had an axe.

Could he do it? Eat his own flesh to survive?

He had to be brave. Grit his teeth. One swing, and he wouldn't starve. The stove would cauterise the wound. Use the rope for a tourniquet.

Light the stove. Heat the plate.

Ready. Let's do it.

Mother's eyes widened.

But the gag muffled her screams.

And in the Darkness, Wake Me
by Jay Faulkner

Every night, in his sleep, he talked, keeping her awake as he tossed and turned throughout his dreams.

It was bad enough listening to him during the day; thirty years together and they'd long run out of things to say.

At night she'd thought she deserved to escape his words, like she'd long ago escaped his embrace.

The pillow, at first, was just to shut him up. She held it over his face and basked in the quiet. No words. Bliss.

She held it there longer. No breath. Silence.

Finally.

She slept.

Until the talking in the darkness woke her.

Spelunking
by Tyler York

Breathe.

Slowly. Steadily.

The flashlight finally flickers off. Bathed in the inky blackness, time stops. *Don't panic.* My body doesn't listen, heart yammering like a drunken prom queen.

Breathe.

Slowly. Steadily.

Someone's coming for me, right?

Drip.

The damned water is going to drive me crazy. I wiggle my fingers to make sure they're still there. I wiggle my toes too.

Breathe.

I suck in the stale air. It sticks to my throat as my lungs try to expand.

I wince.

Slowly. Steadily.

Again, I try to push myself free.

Again, my efforts prove futile.

Nothing to do but wait.

De Muertos
by Jay Alexander

"Take off the mask."

White teeth flashed in the dim light. "You're *insane,*" Miguel spat. Shadows pooled in his eyes.

The stranger leant closer. "Mask. Off."

Outside the grimy windows, the festival was in full swing. White skulls and dark suits bounced in mottled sunlight. Explosions of coloured chalk rocked a surging crowd.

"Mask," the stranger said again. "*Off.*"

And with that, the stranger reached forward, digging the fingers of one hand into Miguel's mouth and pressing a thumb into his right eyeball. He tore outwards.

Miguel's mask was wrenched free, exposing the skull beneath with a spray of crimson.

Lego and Jigsaws
by Ainsley Davidson

You ever step on one of those plastic building blocks? Lego… My kids are always making houses and shit outta them, then leaving them all over the floor.

Fucking hurts, right?

At least this isn't as bad, more a trip hazard than anything.

I flick the light switch and survey the mess they've left out.

Fucking jigsaws. I wouldn't mind if they actually put them back together, instead of leaving the pieces strewn around the lounge.

I fetch rubber gloves and a bag from the kitchen and drop a blood-drenched hand into it as I collect up gory body parts.

The Final Jump Scare
by Tiffany Michelle Brown

"That final jump scare!" Mark performs a chef's kiss. "See why I love this stuff?"

I don't see. The credits roll, a reminder that the story we watched is fiction, but my stomach churns. "I'm not a fan."

"Aw." Mark lassos an arm around me. "Are you scared?"

The blaring soundtrack, all screeching strings, is almost as grating as his patronising question. "I just don't like it. Not my thing."

I snatch up the remote and turn off the TV.

A masked face reflects back at us in the dark reflection of the screen.

I don't have time to scream.

My Treasure
by A.S. Charly

Kyle watched her boyfriend from across the dining table, typing away on his phone.

"Are you happy with me, baby?"

"Eh...sure. Why wouldn't I be?" He didn't even bother looking up.

Knowingly, she smiled and handed him a fancy rose-red cocktail.

"To our eternal love," she said.

Their glasses clinked together.

The knockout drops worked fast. It didn't take long, soon Kyle was lying in a beautiful casket filled with rose pedals. Eyes wide open, but unable to move, he watched how she slowly poured the transparent glittering epoxy resin over him.

"Now you'll forever be mine, my treasure!"

Underground
by Sławomir Mazur

Surprised, he looked around the empty underground station. Only a few minutes left until the last train. Where is everyone?

A strange noise broke the silence. He approached the platform's edge. Maybe it's closed for maintenance?

Two yellow spots appeared in the dark, the noise getting closer. But it didn't sound like wheels rolling on rails, more like quick tapping on a metal surface. A shape emerged from the tunnel.

Yellow spots weren't headlights.

They were eyes.

He didn't have time to escape. The mandible grabbed him, throwing into a giant mouth. Segmented body quickly disappeared down the next tunnel.

Your Nonbinary Nightmare
by Jay Sykes

I have a woman's body. I wish I could tell which woman, so I could give it back. Unfortunately, it's going to rot instead. Unlike that hack, Dr Frankenstein, I intend to inhabit my work.

A lot of my new form is feminine; I do like the curves. The base body I'm using died in a car crash a few months ago. I need a few extra bits here, and the ability to grow hair there, which is where her boyfriend comes in. Same crash, very convenient.

They will be together for as long as I live.

Rather sweet, really.

Roadkill
by Catrin Lawrence

On the dead-grey A49, I see a corpse—half fox, half maggots. It writhes like the possessed's first steps. Mum says, "Don't worry, it's roadkill. Something will eat it."

Trees blur past. A white metal band quarantines the wild.

On a similar road, to a friend's birthday, white streetlight bleeding over me, I wonder what settles for countryside's rot.

Perhaps the other driver wonders too. Too much.

Glass impales me. My friends bleed, broken alongside—death in headlights. No chance for maggots to twitch their guts. Those that settle reach them faster.

Something settles beside me. Something bites. Something feeds.

Koschei's Kurse
by Angel Spencer

Her skin; soft, warm, untouched. It trembles under Koschei's soft, gentle strokes.

"You're mine," he whispers with lustful malevolence.

She whimpers, but it hides her knowing smile.

For she knows his secret. His soul is spellbound—while it's hidden, he can never die.

His hand travels up her bare leg as he breathes on her neck but stops as Georgiy—*her* hero—crashes through the door.

Dagger raised above his head, Georgiy drives it into her heart.

As she—the vessel for Koschei's soul—shudders her last breath, Georgiy sheds a single tear.

Koschei combusts, the spell broken at last.

Portal
by Lindsay Mansfield

Perhaps the summoning had gone wrong: words mispronounced; the wrong planet in retrograde; a virgin sacrifice who had lied. It was more common than not.

He looked through the portal at the creature on the other side. It was far from impressive. Feeble frame, strange eyes, limbs in all the wrong places. Quite pathetic. He almost pitied the poor thing.

As he pushed through the veil, the creature before him began to weep. Such a fool to have summoned him. The Eldritch being coiled a tentacle around the frail human creature, taking great pleasure in his freedom to destroy.

Keep Your Eyes Open, Sweetheart
by Tuesday Fang

He'd participated so willingly. Being trusting, his suspicions hadn't been aroused.

Not like hers.

Martin stood naked against the wall, hands and ankles shackled. Morphine kept him docile—Leonora didn't want noise.

Donning her French maid outfit, she pushed on decorative, sharp talons.

This should excite him. "My gift for you, darling."

Staring at his face, she touched Martin's cheek. Sliding a sharp fingernail under both his eyes, she made red flow. Martin shuddered.

Further jabs to both sides of the neck—dark scarlet spurted.

Bending lower, she plunged deep into his upper groin.

With revenge served, Leonora smiled.

Reciprocate
by Mason Davidson

The creatures were dormant. Soon, they'd feed.

Ronnie, limbs bound, exclaimed, "Babe, I'm sorry! It won't happen again!"

Trish shook her head. "How can I trust you? Cheater! Liar!"

She'd drugged her boyfriend. While Ronnie slept, she'd superglued a shatterproof snorkel mask to his face. But not before trapping a pair of tiny crustaceans beneath the glass.

Trish seethed. "You gave me crabs. I'll give *you* crabs!"

"Babe, please!"

"Wouldn't cry, if I were you. Salty tears might jumpstart their appetites."

It took longer than Trish anticipated, but the hungry critters, nowhere to go, eventually dug into Ronnie's frantic eyes.

The Whispering Wind
by D.M. Burdett

A quiet whine, a soft whoosh; the wind whispers—caressing, cajoling, comforting.

I submit to its whims.

I stand in the shadows, watching and waiting, until the breeze carries commands, vengeful and violent. My eyes alight on the approaching shadow, and the murmuring breaths reach a gusting crescendo.

I reach out as she passes—she cries out in surprise, but my hand covers her mouth. The knife is sharp and quick, and blood runs. She trembles in my arms, her eyes wide.

The wind dies—her final breath—and I look up into accusing faces.

Can't they hear the whispers?

Turn the Handle
by Peter J. Foote

"Quiet, do you want to get caught?" the burglar says.

"Shut up. You said you'd get me into Comeau's shop. Do it! His sausages are destroying my business. I must have his secret," rebuts the butcher.

The door cracks free and two stealthy figures enter Comeau's butcher's shop.

"Help me look for his recipe, I must have it!" the butcher hisses at the burglar.

"I know his secret," and with a stroke of a meat mallet, the butcher is unconscious.

The lights flicker on and Comeau steps in. "Get him onto the counter, it looks like I'm making sausages tonight."

A Zombie's Hunger
by Dusty Burford

There's a smell in the air I can't ignore; it dances on the wind, caresses my senses.

My body tenses. I stop to listen.

Then I see her.

A small child stumbles out of the undergrowth and into the clearing. Ragged clothes hang off her too-skinny frame. Dark circles ring wild eyes, and wet crimson colours her once innocent face.

Moonlight illuminates her graceless fall as she collapses to the ground only steps away, landing with a grunt.

Then she sees me.

But the white-hot compulsion has already enveloped me in its warmth.

She closes her eyes; accepts her fate.

Shattered
by Darlene Holt

She was watching me again, the woman in the window. Crazed, blood-tinted eyes. Cold, haunting smile. Always watching. Judging behind glass.

I saw what she did—cringed, as the kitchen knife punctured his heart, ripping through flesh and bone like paper. Bloody bullets splattered the glass. She glanced toward the window—toward me—as she dragged her husband's corpse across blood-soaked linoleum.

She saw me. She knows I know. And ever since, she won't stop staring. Smirking. Laughing!

I can't take it. I grab the bloody knife and strike the glass and laugh as she shatters into a thousand pieces.

Betrayed
by Jenniefer Andersson

Ruth's hands trembled as she pulled herself up enough to look over the back of the couch, then quickly ducked down again as quietly as she could. She tugged at the sleeping toddler and looked at her sister, who just kept staring dead ahead.

Tapping her sister's knee, Ava barely even looked at her before she did something Ruth would never forget.

Or forgive.

Ava stood up. "We're here." Her voice sounded hollow, devoid of any emotion as she waved her hand.

Gripping her niece, Ruth made a dash for it, her knees weak and hands fumbling for the door.

Silly Old Tree
by Helen M. Merrick

Lucy cowered and clutched the duvet. The tree was hungry again; she was sure of it. Branches clawed at the window and the trunk creaked as if twisting closer, hunting her.

"Oh, darling," said her mother, blithely gazing outside. "It's just a silly old tree on a windy night. Nothing to be—"

With a sudden, tremendous crash, a thick branch pierced the double glazing. It coiled around Lucy's startled mother, twigs burrowing into flesh. Then it swung her against the wall, smashing her skull with a sickening crack.

Lucy stared while the tree retreated with its prey, trailing blood.

Last Night
by Justin Allec

Anette dragged the shotgun by its barrel. The gun's stock bumped from the kitchen's laminate to the living room carpet. Illuminated by the TV's fuzzing static in the living room, Anette faced the boarded-over picture window. It was June, so she imagined her purple irises blooming. Fumbling down the hall to Julie's room for a goodbye kiss, Anette paused in the seashell nightlight's glow. Tears falling, she leaned in for a goodbye kiss and recoiled at her daughter's cold, waxy cheek. No matter; Anette set herself on the edge of the bed and brought the shotgun up to her mouth.

Fruiting Body
by Rowan Bell

I know you're tired. Just climb a little further. Take off those clumsy gloves. That's much easier.

This fork in the tree is perfect. Make yourself comfortable.

Dawn is coming. It will be hot—you should take off your helmet. See, the air here is perfect. The coughing will stop soon.

Take a firm hold of the branches. Nice and tight. Root yourself to the spot.

Can you feel my tendrils lengthening, feeling their way along your airways and nerve fibres, seeking the light?

You gave me warmth, food, a sanctuary in the dark. Now is my time to bloom.

On the Beach
by John C. Mannone

Granular pockets of heat mirage the wavering horizon. Searing light flares on the drying beach, scorching my dark eyes—the cool blue sunglasses protect only for a short while. My skin's covered in white cotton. There is no calming wind, yet waves curl in the singeing sky, from cobalt tint way out to edge of black. I stand on a sloping dune, my telescope stretched out to reach the ebb. I sense the pulse of silent rhythms of the sleeping surf, wonder when this ocean, its quiescence, will awaken as tsunami, its hot cosmic waves rushing to wash me away.

Ritual
by J.M. Faulkner

Donna awakes—fist-bumps her alarm clock which flashes *02:37*—and staggers to the toilet. I'm part dreaming when she returns, but we sleep together—another silhouette tryst.

She withdraws momentarily, nimble in the darkness, and flushes me away. Cleansed, we drift away…

It's *our* ritual.

Tonight, the curtain's ajar. A slither of moonlight touches the duvet. Donna stands at the end of our bed, sheds her nightgown, and sits on my hips.

It's the first I've seen her illuminated like this, and my tongue knots. "…Donna?"

She chuckles, presses a forefinger to my lips, says, "Still in the toilet."

The First Lesson
by Liam Hogan

Emily was trembling as Ben wrapped her fingers around the pistol grip. He could have been annoyed, but he wasn't. The first one was always the hardest. He knew it got easier after that, sometimes so easy you got careless, and got caught, though that was something to be taught another time.

Today's lesson was simple: kill or be killed.

And don't freeze when the moment comes. Don't *doubt*. That's why it was best to start them young.

"Take a breath," he instructed, knife to her throat. "Exhale, and then pull."

His five-year-old daughter carefully nodded and squeezed the trigger.

Hog Roast
by Billie Griffin

Silk rope tightens across breasts; she gasps as he ties the final knot that binds her to bark.

She smiles up at him from beneath ocean eyes as he fingers the rope, admiring the geometry against delicate skin.

He presses a hot kiss to her lips before his tongue traces a wet path from neck to thigh.

A sound in the darkness.

Her breath catches, and she forgets the sweet caress.

An axe swings; he falls silently, hot fluid splashing her nakedness.

Pulling against the restraints, her screams echo through the forest.

"Nice," says the newcomer. "Tie-roast... Just needs stuffing."

Shape Of Death
by Carla Eliot

Shadows tremble at the top of the stairs, weaving together to form an outline of a person.

But this isn't human. Its rotten stench infects the air around me.

I flip the light switch and the shadow retreats. My breath escapes me, and I resume climbing the stairs.

There's a fizzling crackle before the bulb explodes. Bits of glass come raining down, bringing with it the darkness.

I stumble.

Fall.

Fly.

And land on something soft.

Cold realisation creeps over me as I sink into the familiar form beneath me.

The waiting shape at the top of the stairs reappears.

Three Sentence Challenge
by Dawn Burdett

Black clouds billow across the desert as Ben, chanting into the wind in bellows, raises his arms to the skies, summoning the darkest of all dark lords with fire and lightning.

Thunder rumbles, and hairs of white light split the darkness, separating the squall from the swirling dust as Dean rises up from the very depths of the Earth's core and growls upon his subject, "What ungodly thing calls me from my slumber at this time?"

Trembling, pressing a sweaty palm against his keyboard, Ben whispers, terrified, "Tis time to wake, Dark Lord, Bad Romance goes live in twelve hours."

Deathly Voyage
by Zedonk

Manji embarked on a voyage from the shores of Gambia to a port off Nouakchott.

His quest for greener pastures in Europe aboard an inflated rubber raft ended as a suicide mission. They ran out of luck near the Mauritanian shores.

The boat—meant to accommodate a maximum of seventy passengers—was laden with 120. Thus, the vessel experienced a bumpy ride due to tide and overload. It sank, with 80% casualties.

A few survived by a whisker, swimming long distances but losing consciousness. However, Manji survived due to the timely intervention of a rescue team on a patrol boat.

Echelon
by Garrison McKnight

In the aftermath, there was confusion. Strong warriors fought and died in the war, abandoning the young, old, and infirm. The leader chosen was a buffoon, having no sense of honour; only gratifying his needs to be seen, to be exalted.

With the passing years, children grew into adults, learning from the elderly that the Chosen One was not right in the head. We were encouraged to take over, establishing our position in the hierarchy.

Crouching in the ditch, several of us waited for our leader to pass by. His end was near, and we were hungry for his flesh.

Waiting for Santa
by N.E. Rule

Blood drips down into the fireplace, spotting the birch logs. When the moaning stops, I know the trap has finished its job. Looking up into the chimney, I see red velvet and raw bone crushed in the sharpened steel.

The lever releases with a clank, and the freed body falls into the readied funeral pyre. I rip out a tuft of white hair from the snowy beard and place it in my keepsake box along with the mouldy rabbit's foot.

Before lighting the fire, I use the pliers and yank out a front tooth to prepare for my next project.

The Trials of Hunting
by Declan Liam McKendrick

Kneeling before the corpse, I inspect its various wounds.

The lacerations and oversized claw marks are consistent with werewolves, but something feels *wrong*.

The victim is usually left mauled, ripped open, but these strikes are...precise...calculated.

Focusing, I place my hand on its chest, concentrating on its last living Memory.

The man's a hiker? Caught off guard? Knocked down? They're hesitant? They have a goal. A plan?

I return, confused. Why attack like that? Why kill at all? It just leaves evidence…

…That we would have to collect, pinning us to this spot.

Soteria be damned, it's a trap!

A Promised Soul
by Matthew Wallace

The demon felt the gun's metallic scrape as the man shoved it into his own mouth. He pulled the trigger, showering the wall behind him with blood and brain. The demon was reluctantly impressed; no one had ever fought it so hard.

As the man's soul dissolved, the demon appeared in front of a woman who trembled at the sight of it.

"What are you doing here?"

"When you summoned me, you promised a soul. The man you sent me to is gone."

The demon tore into the woman, ripping her soul from her body, and dragging it to Hell.

Whispers
by Erin Jones

She died. My husband's mother.

She hated me.

She's still here, though he doesn't believe me.

The lights flicker.

Her teacup trembles.

I hear her whisper, "Leave!" But only when he is out.

I hear her whisper, "Look!"

Is it my imagination?

Her teacup falls and smashes.

The pieces fly under the closet door.

As I clean it up, I find them in the closet.

Pictures, notes. My husband's rage.

Against other women, against his mother.

Another whisper, "Leave!"

She didn't hate me.

She was trying to protect me.

She helped me find escape.

She found her escape in death.

The Monster
by Nancy Pica Renken

I hate him.

Disgust seethes within me as I crouch beneath the bed. Padding across the carpet, he leaps onto the mattress. Exposed box springs catch, yanking my fur.

Grrr!

He laughs.

My lungs constrict as he body slams into the mattress, flattening me. My claws twitch, itching to rip him to shreds.

I can't.

Flinging his head under the bed, his blue eyes bore into mine. Blonde hair. Eleven years old. He laughs, knowing I can't hurt him.

Once, I wished to be someone else. The monster under the bed became me, and I, him.

I got my wish.

Homeward
by Maxwell Marais

My frostbitten feet ached as I began my long, icy walk. I could count my remaining toes on one hand. My boots were missing patches, *chewed* patches, and I could still recall the taste of leather. But that didn't matter—I was going home. Always best to put the past behind you. Best not to dwell on what happened to the others. Best not to focus on the red-brown stain on my shirt, and the tang of iron in my mouth, and the piece of *skin* still wedged between my teeth. No, none of that mattered. *I was going home.*

Preservation
by Nerisha Kemraj

The smell of iron clogged her nose as Sophie came to. Her face burned, and she couldn't move. A man stood over her, staring.

"Shhh, now, don't scream."

"What's happening? Where am I?"

"I'm sorry the drugs wore off so soon."

Sophie's eyes widened as he drew a bloodied scalpel towards her face.

"Don't touch me!"

"I can't leave you half done, my dear."

Her shrieks reverberated through the room as the scalpel cut into her face.

"I can't let you taint your beautiful skin."

The band on her forehead restricted her as he removed her skin, piece by piece.

Don't Take Me Now
by Oliver C. Seneca

I gasp for air. My lungs clench. The scent of the ancient dead surrounds me as I race through the underground maze, panicking at every turn that leads to no escape. Only countless hollowed eyes stare back at me from the walls as the light of my lantern dances, casting quick shadows along the stacks of bones, stopping at a dead end.

The sounds of brittle feet clicking and clacking echo behind me, but before I can turn to face my mysterious followers, a wave of skeletal hands takes hold of me and drags me back, deep into the dark.

A Murder at Wren Cottage
by Jodie Angell

The wooden doors of Wren Cottage bashed against the walls. The wind whipped. A rat darted across the porch. Pumpkins were split open on the floorboards, their flames diminished.

A fire flickered in the hearth, desecrating a spirit board. A toppled wine bottle lay on the table, leaking its red contents onto the cream carpet.

Ankles bruised, ribs broken, blood oozing from a slash in her neck, Jenny lay dead at the foot of the stairs.

A black being lurked above her, eyes piercing red, drinking her soul. The monster doubled in size, and its cackle rippled through the house.

Thunder
by Duran Blondel

Thunder roars as I wait, the last of me soaking into the muddied battlefield. The war the rages on—deafening and vicious—around me.

My final breaths ache and burn, and I know my time is soon. I peer longingly across the misty field watching for the Valkyries that will surely come to take me to Valhalla; I have lain my life for Odin, for Ragnarok.

But my pain gives way to a single betraying tear and then Freyja comes to me, beckons.

I am not for Folkvangr! Go away!

How can a single tear forsake my life, my sacrifice?

Pop!
by Evan Baughfman

After the party, Carl—wearing his clown make-up—approached one of the guests, a boy, on a secluded road. Carl offered a white balloon.

"More treats this way. Come with me?"

The kid's eyes glowed red. "No, thanks, mister."

Sudden fire raged in Carl's chest. He coughed, spraying blood. Gore dripped down the balloon. Carl gazed upon a Rorschach portrait of his own harlequin visage.

The balloon then inflated. Grew larger. Larger…

Carl shrieked, pressure building inside his skull.

Pop!

Balloon and clown simultaneously burst.

Brains and bone painted the scene.

The boy's eyes dimmed. He made it safely home.

COVID-19 Mantra:
Stay the Fuck at Home
by D. Kershaw

Noise woke him. He scowled into the darkness.

"There's nothing oooooon!" whined a voice.

"There's lots," said another.

"I've watched *all* of Netflix."

"All?"

"Alllllllllll!"

"It's my turn to choose," interrupted a third. "Ru Paul's Drag Race!"

"No!" chorused the others.

Jeremiah rose—his feet left no prints in the dust—and transcended from attic to lounge. The Pottock family fled in fear, screams echoing.

* * *

Shouting woke him. He scowled into the darkness.

Jeremiah rose—no breath parted cobwebs—and transcended from attic to lounge.

"Don't scowl, Jeremiah," said Mrs Pottock, her spectral form shimmering. "It's your fault we're here."

Esser
by Robin Braid

The great, white moon flickered high above the world as a dark, crooked finger swept hair from the boy's eyes. His father turned away, unwilling to watch the jagged, ravenous maw close around his sweet head with a sickening crack. Blood ran south, the boy fell limp and the beast's form swelled.

A sob from the kneeling crowd elicited a glare from the beast that summoned silence. The broken remnants of the boy were tossed to the dirt and a young girl, hand in hand with her mother, slowly shuffled forward.

A slick, serpentine tongue writhed across bloodied lips, "More."

Unholy Transaction
by Burr Nadette

The wind brought his scent, heady and beautiful, and it wrapped around me like a heavy blanket, muffling the street sounds and enveloping me in its embrace. I tried to ignore the mounting pressure within, but my skin crawled with wonting. I stepped out of the alley as he approached.

"How much?" he asked before following me back into the darkness.

His hands ran over my body as he thrust, and I pulled him close, my lips grazing his neck. As he reached his climax, I sank my teeth and gulped from the pumping vein, my own desire finally satiated.

Mammon
by D.B. Morvid

The ritual begins with the lighting of blood candles.

Four cloaked figures begin to chant.

She stares at me with hate-filled eyes, breath coming in short gasps.

I draw the sharp edge of a dagger across my palm. Strapped to the slab, she is helpless as my blood flows over her face and body. Her screams become part of the spell. Her fear calls to the demon, Mammon.

I smile as I plunge the blade into her chest.

She gurgles her last breath before smoke rises from her mouth. Our master now has a new host in my mother's shell.

Red Red Wine
by S.J. Townend

Bryan steps into the confession booth.

"Father, forgive me. I've sinned."

"What've you done?"

"Ungodly relations. My wife's younger sister. And brother."

"Thirty Hail Marys. Drink the blessed wine."

A bony hand slides a chalice of red, warm liquid through the small hatch.

"Certainly, Father. Thank you."

Bryan necks the pungent drink and exits the booth, staggering. He sees Father chatting to an elderly woman at the far end of the church.

"Father— Wh-who did I confess to?" he says, panicking.

"No idea," Father replies.

Bryan falls, lips a-froth with warm red lace, eyes rolling, body convulsing. In seconds, dead.

Date Night
by L.N. Hunter

Pitch-black.

Groggy, you grope for the door.

Locked.

Your cries wither—throat's too dry.

Think! Party… Drinking with Daniel. Then—

Light flares. A silhouette fills the doorway.

"Where am I?" you croak. "Where's Daniel?"

The stranger leaves a glass of water and retreats, locking you in.

You break the glass, wait with a fragment in your bleeding hand.

When your jailer returns, you slash him, shove past, and flee.

Screeching brakes. A car door thuds.

Daniel!

"There's a man… He—"

Daniel clutches you tight—too tight.

"So, you met my brother." He grins and drags you back to your prison.

Spilt Syrup
by Lane Jordan

"Please excuse me, I don't know why I'm crying."

The two cops exchange looks.

"That's alright. Your neighbour called in a disturbance. Do you recall what happened?"

"My husband and I had breakfast. He left for work. I took my tea into the garden."

"Are you sure, Mrs Evers?"

"Yes."

The officer raises an eyebrow, surveys the scene behind her—the table strewn with congealing eggs and spilt coffee, and Mr Evers facedown on a pillow of pancakes in a sticky pool of maple syrup and blood.

She looks up, dabbing her eyes. "Sorry, I don't know why I'm crying."

This Wretched Soul
by Eddy Vegas

Gagging on the filthy rag stuffed inside my mouth

Only pitiful whimpering escapes my throat.

The darkness mocks as my belly spews fresh, warm blood.

This time it's the rats they send to feast on my steaming organs, and oozing puss from festering wounds.

Kidnapped for revenge, then abandoned to my fate.

I no longer fear what monsters lurk in the shadows.

Like me, they hunt in the night—vigilantes some say—leaving me to rot upon this hook, like their victims before me.

My belly aches as entrails unwind, slowly spilling to the filthy floor.

Emptying…like my hope.

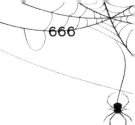

Ice Queen
by Shawn M. Klimek

Their hearts had once beat as one, aflame with hot-blooded passion—but no more. Whereas his love persisted, it had become unrequited.

Clutching her hand, he begged, his voice breaking, "Don't you feel anything?"

She gave no reply, only stared back at him, sneering. She didn't care if he suffered. Her heart had grown empty, her blood as cold as her icy gaze. His only solace was that she no longer appeared to hate him. When he finally accepted that her mind would never be changed, he stashed her hand alongside the rest of her and shut the freezer door.

Watermark
by Mel Mulrooney

Bottles littered the table, wine spilling onto the floor. She sank down, reaching for a moment of peace. She wanted to forget. To be elsewhere. To be nowhere.

A small spot grew on the ceiling. She watched it spread, reminded of the inkblot tests at the hospital. Two people fighting. A menacing beast. Death and more death.

Water dripped onto her face. Dammit, Johnny! She told him a hundred times not to leave the tap running!

No.

Johnny was dead. Not Johnny.

More drops fell. She smelled copper. Fingers traced the sticky smear on her skin.

Oh, God!

Not water.

His Bite's Worse than His Bark
by Gregg Cunningham

"That's just wrong, dude." Nick retched, feeling nauseous again, as the dog on the ground whimpered by the sheriff's lifeless body.

"Just kill the poor fucker and be done."

"No way!" Devlin spat, shaking his wounded hand. "I'm gonna make it suffer." He slid the hunting knife across another exposed tendon as the dog fought frantically against its bindings, wriggling against the duct tape wrapped around its snout.

"Dammit, let's get the hell out of here before anyone else comes."

Delvin sneered, staring into the Alsatian's petrified wide eyes as the blood oozed onto the grass.

"Guard dog, my arse."

Soul Cat
by Diane Arrelle

Jeremy stared into the cat's eyes, forcing himself not to blink. Perspiration beaded on his forehead from the effort.

The cat effortlessly stared back.

As sweat rolled into his right eye, Jeremy cursed the briny sting that forced his eyes shut.

He heard the cat purr.

Damned thing knew it had won. Again. The beast bested him all five rounds.

Blinking his eyes open, Jeremy asked, "Best of eleven?"

In answer, the cat's razor-sharp teeth fastened onto his throat. Struggling to pull the demon creature off, Jeremy's last thought was, *Really bad idea, holding a staring contest with a Hellcat.*

The Sound
by Tim Law

That sound.

Thwack. Thwack.

I know not if I am awake or dreaming. It has infiltrated my every moment. I hear it now—a slow, steady, rhythmic repetition. It is part *crack*, part *squelch*; a sound that churns my stomach each time I hear it. I try to force my ears to keep the sound at bay, but it is impossible. Over and over again, I hear the cleaver fall. Sometimes it is accompanied by the grunt of effort. The wielder is strong, but some men have thick skins.

It is the sound of my father, "The Butcher", busily working.

Still Afraid
by Joshua D. Taylor

After watching fifty people get fed to a giant disembodied mouth, I thought I would no longer be afraid. Not the case. I pissed myself and blubbered like a baby when the bald cultists in coveralls dragged me over. They swung me by my arms and legs, then tossed me into the giant mouth, afraid to get too close. I was terrified when the huge, bruised and blood-stained lips gently parted, permitting my entry. I was still horrified beyond rational thought as the massive yellow teeth splintered my bones like toothpicks, shredded my flesh, and burst my organs like balloons.

Fools Wish
by J.C. Haggerty

I patted the dirt as my eyes darted down each road. I ensured I was at the centre of the crossroads with my most prized possession lying beneath the earth.

A voice crowded me. "One wish."

I blanked and sputtered, "I want to be a mermaid."

There was a long, mournful sigh as my legs fused. Blood dripped from my fingers. Scales poked out of my skin. Air refused to enter my lungs as I gagged for breath. My tail flapped, half-formed, before my body stilled.

Death came for me, searing words onto my soul. "Fool be the mortal tongue."

Gore May Delight
by Steven Holding

As born connoisseurs, their refined palates always craved the latest taste sensations. From bison to venison, they hadn't yet met a meat that they couldn't appreciate when prepared correctly.

The aroma rising from the sizzling pan set their senses alight. Garnishing the dish lightly, chef flipped the portions onto plates, serving them to each eagerly awaiting guest.

Of those attending the dinner party, none were strangers to the partaking of human flesh. After much experimentation, they'd finally concluded that, just like the divine difference between veal and beef, the most succulent cuts were indeed the youngest.

But baby's *always* best.

Mother
by Finnian Burnett

Steve opens the door, exhaustion in his sunken eyes. Years of caring for mother live on his face.

"She's dead, then," I say.

"Dead, yes."

I follow him to the dining room. *Drag, thump*. His lame leg scrapes the floor, his other foot stomps in compensation.

"For real this time*?*"

He nods without turning.

She's seated at the table. A spike protrudes from her chest.

I need to know. My fingers fumble for her wrist, seeking the warm thumping pulse. Nothing. It's done then. Relieved, I turn to hug my brother. As I do, mother's voice croaks. "Welcome home, Janey."

The Christmas Killer
by Joshua Greally

The Christmas Eve cold froze my soul.

When Francine got home, she hugged Johnathan and passionately kissed his "father," James, before heading upstairs to shower.

An open window allowed easier access than a chimney. She only saw me as the knife pierced her back, her blood staining my shirt red.

In the downstairs kitchen James prepared cookies and milk. His arterial spray soaked my beard.

Finally, I went into the living room where Johnathan lay. A squeaky floorboard betrayed me.

"Santa." He ran to me. His parent's blood bonded us together as we hugged. My knife pressed against his back.

The Whispering
by Lyndsey Croal

Hush now, listen to the whispering of the moor. You can think of nothing else as you walk, footfall light on boggy ground.

Ahead is a tall ring of umbrella-shaped flowers. A musty scent fills the air, drawing you in. It clings to your throat until you can no longer breathe, no longer speak.

The whispering intensifies. Then you're falling, headfirst, into the plant ring. But you don't hit the ground. Your body becomes weightless.

The whispering echoes inside your head. And now you recognise it. Your own voice.

"Hush now," it says. "Listen to the whispering of the moor."

On Social Media
by Jean Marţin

No officer, my husband wasn't murdered.

He couldn't have been. I'm not married.

I wrote a story about a woman who was afraid of her basement. Her husband wasn't, and he was murdered there one night. I wrote it in the first person.

The publisher put it on my social media, including Neighbor2Neighbor, with the lost dogs and yard sales. A lot of people saw it there. Someone must have thought it was real.

No one was murdered in my basement.

You can look there if you like. I won't go down there at night, but you have a gun.

Atomic Soup
by Dana Branch

The vessel came to a deafening, juddering stop in churned up red desert, and Harrison opened his eyes and looked around.

Still alive!

The rest of his crew weren't so lucky. He stepped over Smith's decapitated head as he pushed his way out of the decimated ship.

His heads-up display identified a habitable environment, and he removed his helmet.

His skin blistered and burst, the radiating heat turning him into atomic soup in milliseconds.

* * *

Leader Seven of Planet Urtta congratulated Private 608 on his burgeoning mind-control skills as Harrison's crew in the undamaged spacecraft watched Harrison's empty spacesuit fall over.

Feast
by August Quinn

Ethel's childhood had been spent happily in the rocky dwelling and muddy fields. Lashing rain and wild winds stirred, but inside, the family was cosy as can be.

Presently, they sat down to dinner.

Ethel, not invited, found that the warm glow from the windows brought with it a certain half-remembered sting. Upon the table, among the carrots, peas, and potatoes—some of Ethel's most favourites—was a pork roast. And what a sight it was!

But there was to be no feast for Ethel, and no welcoming home.

Ethel's heart ached—figuratively, of course.

The storm prevailed, and the family ate Ethel.

One Last Bite
by Gary McDonough

Endless hunger is all that fills my grumbling insides right now. I'd do anything for just one more meal, one last bite, another tasty morsel. Wandering the land aimlessly in constant search for sustenance. My emaciated body wasting away, never able to feel satisfaction. Tireless, bleeding feet providing perpetual motion. After consuming my beloved wife and children, I deserted my family home, finding myself here.

Lost…

Alone…

Daily existence becoming more challenging as my body deteriorates.

Skin and bone.

Mother often said, "You can rest when you're dead!"

Unfortunately, rest proved to be a tormenting luxury I would never experience.

Revenge is Mine
by Paula R.C. Readman

Woken by the smell of blood, I push aside the leaves covering me. Staggering forwards the stench of reprisal drives me crazy. Trapped without a soul, neither dead nor alive, I sniff the air, wanting to taste the blood of my murderer. He used my body, discarding it like a rag doll in the woods. With no trace of humanity left, I seek revenge.

Through the window, I slip, dirt and worms tumble from me. He sleeps so peacefully until I deliver him to hell. Tearing into his flesh with bony hands and teeth, I rip out his beating heart.

Early Morning Coffee
by Benjamin Goldstein

I walked to the bedroom holding a steaming cup of coffee. The early grey morning light filtered in through the blinds and illuminated the curled-up form of my wife under the blankets. I smiled and placed the coffee on the bedside table.

"I love you, honey. Your coffee's here when you get up."

A blanket-covered arm patted me on the leg affectionately. I smiled wider and walked back into the hall to see the shocked face of my wife staring at me from the kitchen.

"Who were you talking to?" she asked as I heard the bed creak behind me.

Music
by D. Day Bryan

My family surrounds me, but they are just a dim glow, a quiet, babbling brook of muted sound; I can only hear the harps.

Ethereal music fills my consciousness. Wings fill my vision. I smile, because I know it's time, I know what will become of me; these angelic beings will take me to *Heaven*.

I see a flash of ebon and feel a whisper's touch of feathers on my skin, and I turn my smiling face.

"Is it time?" I ask.

With a hand signal, the director cuts off the melody and turns to me.

Lucifer smiles. "It is."

Sweet as Could Be
by Patrick Winters

She was the sweetest thing around. Everybody who knew her said as much. And was it any wonder? After all, her parents named her Candy, of all things. And it fit her so very well.

Skin softer than angel food cake. Eyes as brown and creamy as Cadbury chocolate. Lips so red and lush, like the finest liquorice.

Hell, even the chunks of her brain looked like fresh sorbet, as he'd found out when he bashed her skull in with his hammer.

It made him wonder if she tasted as sweet as she seemed?

Perhaps just a nibble to see...

First to Go
by Michelle Brett

It started out as just a prick, like a needle piercing the skin. But then the pain began.

It radiated from his stomach. An intense burning that tore through his frame. Fingers worked to locate the source, only to clasp upon a protruding object.

Warm liquid dripped from the cold steel and pooled on the wooden floorboards below.

Then a chill emerged, a welcomed relief. It dulled his senses, even as the knife was torn from his flesh. Black spots appeared as his legs finally gave way.

Darkness. His last words repeating.

"It's just a noise. Nothing to worry about."

Bunny Butcher
by Daytona Bulove

Teeth tore at flesh, meting the fatal wound.

Buffy Bunny grinned, white teeth stained carmine by the life juice of her enemy. Her brown fur, matted in gore, stuck up in peaks all over her little body. As her eyes swept over the ruined rabbit, satisfaction seeped into her very core, and she breathed a triumphant but exhausted sigh.

She pulled the leg of her once nemesis, dragging the body in through the warren's entrance.

Piles of putrefying flesh, eviscerated entrails, and splintered bones littered the dirt floor, and she added the limp leporid.

"I really must get better storage."

Stowaway
by Kat Friday

Seven-year-old AJ snuck into the sleigh, hoping to soon see the North Pole and its various wonders. The elves! The toy factory! Polar bears!

When Santa squeezed out of a neighbour's chimney, AJ crouched lower, behind massive bundles of tethered gifts.

Santa buckled himself in tight, then grabbed the reins of his magical deer.

AJ smiled. They were off, rocketing into the sky at incredible speed! Unimaginable, dizzying speed, AJ discovered.

Within seconds, the boy puked and blacked out. Freezing winds flung him, unnoticed, from the sleigh.

Weeks later, he was found mangled atop a skyscraper, nineteen miles from home.

Homeward Bound
by Keith R. Burdon

On a straight road through the woods, dead life is starting to accumulate on the windscreen. Tiny visceral explosions. He feels sadness—an insect is still a living thing after all. How odd to feel such melancholy when he is surrounded by nature's splendour.

His hand reaches for the wipers, then hesitates. Clearing the remains from existence seems somehow disrespectful. Like they never were.

He puts his hand back on the wheel for now. His father's words are never far away: *ten and two; eyes on the road.*

A muffled scream from the trunk interrupts his train of thought.

Into the Deep
by John Ward

She gasped as cold, dark water enveloped her. Her arms flailed. Her chest burned, and when she saw the heavy chain twisted around her legs, she wanted to scream.

Azure became indigo as she descended. Strange, curious fish nibbled at her clothing. Her chest pain was now white hot. Her head felt heavy and ready to explode. Precious gas bubbles seeped from her pursed lips, and she wondered if she would pass out. She looked up at the pinprick of distant sunlight. She tasted salty fluid and her lungs erupted in an effervescent froth.

She surrendered herself to the white.

The List
by Charles Welch

My grocery list for next week:

Carrots, apples, tea, rice cakes, multigrain bread, chunky peanut butter, radishes, pepperoni log, spicy peppers, lemons, hot sauce, chips and dip,

Maxi pads, panties, pantyhose, socks, golf balls, baseballs, condoms, depilatory cream,

Roofing nails, silicone in a tube with a gun, bleach, ammonia, rubbing alcohol, hydrogen peroxide, vinegar, duct tape, zip ties,

Hobby knife set, syringes, small kettle grill, camera, sleeping bag, trash bags, pick, shovel,

(Do Not Buy All This In One Place!)

Portable DVD player with a good speaker, cartoon DVDs, chocolate milk, ice cream and candy, lots and lots of candy

Stillness
by Connor Sassmannshausen

The dripping of my blood echoes through the cell as I wake from my latest brush with unconsciousness. Pain rolls through my entire body. My jailers certainly know how to cause pain.

The air is still, not even the smallest shift around my chained form. Stillness, solitude, peace.

They want information about my organisation, because we fight them. I'd rather die than give anyone up.

It's only a matter of time before they go too far, and I don't wake.

I feel the air shift with the slightest breeze. Here they come. Maybe I'll die this time. One can hope.

The Summoning
by David Jobe

Viscera dripped from the dagger before it plunged into the exposed heart. The dying man gurgled, blood oozing from his mouth. Inside his open chest cavity, the vital organs quivered as the brain gave one last order. Even the large intestines—some looped out over the bound man's arms, and slowly crawled down the altar's sides, ceased in their twitching.

"Baphomet, we summon thee!" thirteen witches chanted in unison, faces to the sky.

The corpse turned its head, a smirk on its twisted face. "I was already here." Black oily tendrils slipped out from the corpse's wounds.

The screaming began.

In the Sack (With the Necrophiliac)
by Den Ghostliven

"A VIRUS!" cried the news.

"RABIES, MAYBE…"

Always obsessed with the cold kiss of death, he decided to utilise the crisis to grant an unfulfilled wish. With the bodies piling higher, it was time to feel a corpse's caress and satiate his desires.

When the girl next door became another casualty, he couldn't ignore it.

With her bound and gagged, he succeeded in beginning the deed. It was better than anything he'd ever dreamed of.

Finally spent, he dozed off in bed.

Then awoke bleeding; found himself screaming.

She'd escaped.

And who'd have guessed that the dead could give head?

The Contract
by Jocanada Beckwith

My transformation is nearly complete.

A grotesque black claw reaches out and digs into the flesh of my forehead. Searing pain shoots through me as the Master of Hell erases the mark of my baptism. My name is struck from the Book of Life, rewritten in the Book of Death. I am now Hated One and live soulless amongst you.

You see me everywhere.

Sometimes shunned and ignored, sometimes lauded and adored. At all times, entering your mind, removing your own self and soul and replacing them with whatever takes my fancy: Avarice, Ignorance, Anger, Obsession, Lechery, Envy and Disease.

The Hungry Catacomb
by Victor Nandi

"Like it here?"

Yvette frowned. "It's scary."

Marcel wrapped his arms around her from the back. "But nobody's around." He started kissing behind her ear, his fingers playing on her neck.

Yvette's uneasiness began to melt away. Eyes closed, she moaned as those hands ran over her body, caressing her, holding her tighter, drawing her closer and closer to the wall.

* * *

"Stay together. It's easy to get lost arou—" The guide stopped suddenly.

The tourists halted and gaped at the shrivelled remains of a couple caged behind a mesh of skeletal arms jutting out of the ancient catacomb's wall.

Cornered
by Peter Caffrey

Her eyes rolled back; pure white orbs flecked with a filigree of red veins. Her tongue flickered, tasting the air. She had sensed my presence.

In the darkness of my hiding place, I felt every cut on my body, each incision oozing coagulated blood and viscous pus. Nausea overwhelmed me, cramps sending sharp pulses of agony through my guts. It was only the adrenalin keeping me conscious—but for how much longer?

As she crept towards me, her lithesome limbs flexing like a predatory arachnid, a single thought echoed in my head.

There were so many worse ways to die.

Last One
by Gordon Dunleavy

I've avoided the monster so far, but my luck is running out. I don't mind dying. I'll actually be glad when it's all over—then I won't have to worry anymore. I know how it kills, how it eats. I know what type of pain to expect, but how do I prepare myself for the excruciating kind?

It's at my door now. I hear its footsteps, feel its evilness. I hide under what's left of my grandpa. Hoping it won't see me again. But I'm the last one alive.

I won't scream like the others.

I'm not worried.

It's time.

Outrunning the Bear
by Kevin David Anderson

When the zombie apocalypse happened, it wasn't like those old Romero movies. They could run. Really haul. Bullets, even headshots, just pissed them off.

Why did Richard and I even bring guns? Track team conditioning kept us ahead of them, but we hadn't any food. We got weaker, slower. They got closer, and I knew they'd catch me. Richard sprinted yards ahead as I felt Zombies touch my collar. My first thought was to put a bullet in my head, then, another idea.

After shooting Richard's leg I never turned back. The only thing that followed me was his screams.

Scarecrow
by Cassandra O'Sullivan Sachar

The bikers strung him up in the field that night—tied him to a post, the rope so tight it chafed his wrists.

James's whole body ached from the repeated blows rained down upon him. They each took a turn: a slap, kick, or punch. He must have a concussion, a broken rib.

Shivering under the October sky, he waited for them to return and release him. This was the initiation, right? They wanted him in. Right?

Blood dripped down his face until it froze in the moonlight. And James died alone amongst the cornstalks, unable to escape.

Forgotten. Dismissed.

1,000 Cuts
by G. Allen Wilbanks

With delicate precision, she traced the scalpel through one of the few remaining patches of intact skin. It parted easily against the razor's edge.

Her victim coughed, gagged, then ceased breathing altogether.

"Dammit!" she cursed, quietly. She held out the bloody blade to her sister, who was laughing at her failure. "673. Can you beat it?"

Adorned in identical blue surgical scrubs, her younger sibling accepted the proffered tool and turned excitedly toward the bound, wide-eyed young man on the table next to her. She lowered the scalpel to begin her first incision.

"We'll find out," her sister replied. "One..."

The Cold People
by Fiona M. Jones

"Welcome to Goldstone Cryonic Facility," I said in my most professional voice. "I'll give the three of you a brief tour before we discuss your contract."

The client and his daughter nodded. She turned his wheelchair to follow me, her child trotting alongside.

"Is that why you call it cryonic?" the granddaughter asked. "Because of the people crying?"

"No, no," I assured her. "Crying? Nobody's crying!"

She stared at me. "The thin grey people, walking in circles, waiting."

"W-waiting?"

"The cold people." She gestured around us. "Can't you see them crying?"

I lost that sale. People shouldn't bring small children.

The Quiet Aquarium
by Diana Allgair

Roy, the aquarium's nighttime janitor, limped past rows of dimly lit tanks. Blue light reflected from the water and danced across the empty room. With one hand, the janitor dragged a vacuum behind him.

As he adjusted the music playing through his headphones, Roy missed the opening and closing of a lid. He did not hear the wet slapping of tentacles as they slid over one another.

There was no mess, no splotch of red, to indicate foul play. The lid slid back to its rightful place. And then it watched for another and waited, just as it always had.

The 365th Day
by Scott McGregor

On the 365th day, I returned to the ruined world. Months spent hidden, weeks of praying, now I emerged, a graveyard of bones beneath my feet. The land, enveloped by ash, the sky, blackened by smoke, a world prone to darkness.

And within the darkness, they lurked. They, who arose after the world ended. They, who scoured in packs throughout the night. They, who devoured anyone that crossed their path. They, who resembled people, the subterranean doppelgangers of the hidden world.

They, the Shadownborne.

On the 365th day, I returned to the ruined world and joined the graveyard of bones.

Subterranean Loser
by Maxine Churchman

The phone battery dies, plunging you into complete darkness.

Heart pounding, eyes wide but useless, you stumble on, a hand on each side of the tunnel—the walls are slimy.

The noise comes again. You whip your head around, trying to determine whether it's ahead or behind. But sound is deceptive; you can't tell.

Shivering and sweating, you increase your pace.

You sense movement behind—a sharp pain is followed by paralysis.

Dragged to its lair, unable to scream—the agony of each incision and insertion is suffered in silence.

Your warmth incubates its young. Your flesh will satisfy their birthing hunger.

Abducted
by Arlo Gorevin

"Aliens around here," the old man at the garage had said, but they'd laughed and drove on, until the lights came from the sky and the car came to a sudden stop. The tall figures in silver clothes and visored helmets pulled her and the boy from the car, shouting at them in odd metallic crackles.

They strapped her to a cold metal table next to the boy, and she screamed as they dissected him, examining organs speared on thin silver rods.

When they turned to her, the old man lifted his visor and told her she should have listened.

Torment
by Lauraine S. Blake

Bars. Iron, dark, and savage cold, obscure me.

They part with a great creaking and clanking. Then my body is drawn on. Though, perhaps, it's not mine at all, but theirs. I am a creature—their creation—naught but blood and pain.

An amalgamation.

The rack calls. Then the whips do. They scour, slice—shred. Ripping savage wails from my flesh and I yield my dignity to the night, howling like the ebony wind.

Pain eviscerates me; shatters me, as hammers shatter bone; knives shatter flesh. And I am done. A pallid spectre screaming at the dawn, bloodless and alone.

The Witch's Heart
by Stephanie Simmone

I clutched the blade with trembling fingers, cold steel in my palm. My eyes darted around. Shadows seemed to come alive, mocking my fear. I was taking a walk in the forest when everything went dark and silent. Even the moon was hiding. I stumbled upon the witch, and watched, frozen, as she killed a man, ripped his heart clean out, sucked the blood from the organ, and cackled into the night.

As I hid, I tried to calm my laboured breath and racing heart that played the music of my doom. Then, right beside me, she laughed.

I cried.

Sacrifice to the Moloch
by Darkbird Bat

Wind whistled through the trees, rustling branches—eerie sounds in the moonless night. Silent shadows huddled together, their steps a steady rhythm to Tophet.

Candles flickered in the breeze.

Abijah stood in line, motionless bundle in his arms, trying to hide his dirty tears—he didn't want to anger Kronos.

When it was his turn, Abijah held the child aloft for Kronos to see.

Kronos' bronze face was impassive.

Abijah tenderly placed the bundle in Kronos' hand. It rolled, shroud unwrapping, into the fiery pit below.

"I see your tears, Abijah," boomed Kronos.

Mothers wept—it would mean more sacrifices.

The Grave Robber
by Jasmine Jarvis

"Don't disturb the grave of the Ghoul" is the townsfolks' warning about the grave of the Baroness.

I only care for the jewels that adorn her wealthy corpse.

After a while of digging, I wipe the sweat from my brow and reach for the lantern, shining its light into the pit.

I realise, in horror, a pale face is staring up at me, sharp, jagged teeth bared. Moving with supernatural speed, she grabs me, and bites down into my shoulder, tearing flesh, causing me to spasm in agony.

My screams echo across the old graveyard as she eats me alive.

To Keep Someone's Heart
by Chris Bannor

Jessie loved stuffed animals. Every birthday, every Christmas, every holiday in-between, people bought her stuffed animals. She never had too many, and she loved them all.

Jessie loved the feel of her plastic knife ripping through the strings that held arms and eyes in place. She loved putting her hand inside to pull the stuffing out before she added crayon-drawn organs. She loved stitching them up again with her needle.

Dad taught her best. After all, he was the one who took Mama apart and taught Jessie the only way to keep someone's heart was to dig it out yourself.

Awaiting My Saviour
by K. Wren Reeds

My eyes focus on the red and blue *wau kucing* on the fin upon which I float, but my mind flashes back to the moment of impact.

The fear, the panic. Screaming of jet engines. One final explosion as we hit the water.

I'd searched the depths for my daughter, hallucinating: first her beautiful blonde hair; then feral-toothed shadows.

My only solace is it would have been quick—she couldn't swim.

Fresh water ran out three days ago. I don't have long. Convinced my saviour will come, I cling to my boarding pass as tears drip from my nose.

MH370.

Unanswered Prayers
by Jacqueline Moran Meyer

Clumps of skin, hair, and ripped fingernails littered the floor around the bed where the corpse lay.

The priest's slick hands had made squeezing the woman's throat difficult.

Exhausted, he went into the bathroom to wash up and practice his lies to the family.

"She defeated Satan and is with almighty God," he would say.

This usually was followed by a "Thank you, Father," before he skipped back to the parish.

After exiting the bathroom, the empty bed puzzled him.

Hearing a woman's laugh above him, the priest peered up at the ceiling.

His first and only prayer went unanswered.

Human Warmth
by Bridget Haug

Glancing at the cashier's name tag, I place the items on the counter. Biscuits, canned fish, a kitchen knife.

"How's it going, Betty?" I ask.

No answer. I know what she sees; grey hair, tired skin, dried sweat on unwashed clothes. It's been months since someone said my name.

I pay with the only credit card I still have. Not for long.

It's dark outside. People walk past me, their faces tight. I pull the knife out, sink the blade deep into a man's gut. Warm blood covers my hand and I smile.

Soon, they will all say my name.

Together Forever
by Tammy Bird

The shadow moved when she moved.

It wasn't her. It was broader, more masculine than her slight form could ever create. "I should fear you," she whispered.

It consumed her skin, slowly, methodically. *And yet, you don't.*

It was right. She welcomed the burning of her flesh, the hints of death, as the darkest parts of the shadow began to nibble.

You have to let me in.

She sucked a ragged breath through bloodied lips.

The shadow swirled through—its heat briefly awful, then blissfully calm inside her mouth.

She exhaled a tawny puff of smoke-like air.

They were one.

A Day at the Sea Park
by Sheri White

The manatee drew big crowds, as did the killer whale. The front row loved it when Ramu would saturate them with seawater.

Then a tragedy changed it all.

Much later, the investigation would reveal someone had taken an axe to the wooden rollercoaster track.

Bodies splattered to the ground; some landing in the aqua theatre tank, the blood driving the killer whale into a frenzy, turning the water a pastel pink.

Crazed, the whale killed its trainer, pulling her down to the bottom of the tank. The audience stampeded, crushing slower runners.

Only one person stayed in their seat, smiling.

Breathe
by Delfina Bonuchi

My lungs burned, arms flailed, head pounded, but she just watched from afar as I writhed.

Breathe.

Her dark eyes—ebon pools—pleaded, but her smile was wide, sharp teeth glinting in the diffused light.

Breathe.

I reached out, movements slow and tortured, but she dodged and dived, fins flashing.

Breathe, she whispered without words from close behind, just as darkness began to curl at the edges of my world.

Breathe, she bellowed, face close to mine, and I sucked in a great lungful of salty water.

Then, as I closed my eyes one last time, she finally kissed me.

The Hunger
by Sundae Iris

The rat scuttling across the cellar floor startles when I rise from the soiled mattress, chains rattling.

Then a smile paints its furry face—it *knows*.

My dreams are filled with the taste of its juicy body—it's a constant phantom memory.

I look at the crimson pool that spreads from 'neath my captor's head and salivate. The rickety stairs are my saviour and my downfall—no one comes when I scream. Not even him.

The rat, atop the greying face, pauses its wet gnawing to watch my tormented tears.

It's a year since I turned. I'm so fucking hungry.

Beast
by Bex Pinckney

Snow falls. The beast wanders the streets of his mind, hiding in darkened alleyways and corners. He accepts the presence of the creature as it takes the innermost parts of him, transforming what was once pure into soiled linens, blowing in the harsh blizzard. Humanity doesn't have a place here. Instead, there are teeth stained with the blood of those the monster has devoured, sharpened from filing on bones, perfect for tearing into the flesh of others that breaks so easily. He gives in, feeding the beast victim after victim as he sharpens his own teeth, preparing for the hunt.

Last Meal
by Guy Riessen

The cruise ship sinks fast.

Trapped below with water flooding in, I swim through mangled bodies washing through corridors.

I find the couple in a cabin mostly filled with water, but with air trapped by a bulkhead. She claws, screaming as I pulp his face against the steel walls. Her, I hold under until the bubbles stop.

The leg stump of gnawed flesh floats back up. I push it down, out through the tear in the ship's hull. No one will look for human bite marks. An air pocket this size should last me until the body recovery divers arrive.

Hide and Seek
by Constantine E. Kiousis

The girl crouched in a shadowed corner, face bloodied as she watched her bedroom door crack open. Soft, amber light bled in as a shape stalked inside, the glint of a kitchen knife flashing against the moonlight.

"Sweetheart?" the man whispered, panting. "It's alright, I won't hurt you."

The child observed as he crept past her before lunging onto his back. Her father's screams filled the air as sharp teeth tore at the flesh of his neck, and dark crimson spurted from the gash as she feasted until he fell silent.

Your brother next, the voice slithered in her mind.

Blood Angel
by T.A. Arnold

I flap my arms and legs, snow angel style, laughing at the slosh of the warm, thick liquid surrounding me. Licking my lips, a groan of appreciation rumbles from my chest as I savour the heavenly taste of the sanguine fluid. Four figures hang above me, in order of height, dripping the essence of their lives into the pool surrounding me.

The youngest whimpers, tears cascading down her face as her blue eyes find mine. "Please, Daddy. Why?" she cries, her tiny nine-year-old body trembling.

I turn to her with a macabre grin, "Because you should have never been born."

Count Backwards from Ten
by Blaise Langlois

Beep...beep...beep. The steady muted tones call her back from the dark ether, the cloying smell of anaesthetic mixing with rubber. Her throat, constricted, she has an overwhelming sense of fullness.

Muffled voices undulate in her ears, as if under water.

A burning trail blazes across her abdomen. Pressure. She cannot scream as her viscera are shifted and pulled from her body. She senses blood exiting, the coppery scent almost overpowering her senses—instead, pain dominates. A fire spreads, her nerves electric. Feeling as though her skin is being turned inside out—

"We've lost her, Doctor."

Visage
by Christy Brown

The once white dress, tinged yellow with time, hung from her gaunt frame. Standing before the demonic mirror, she eyed the pallid image of her face with sympathy and longing. Her servitude was etched within this reflection, and there was no hope of escape.

On her side of the mirror, she awaited the next victim upon whom she would mete an assault. The mirror would soon deliver a soul: a worthy opponent.

Until her collection counted complete, she would wait in an endless eternity. An eternity that began the day she donned the enchanted dress: the armour of her Lord.

From Gretel's Watch
by August van Stralen

The old lady sits in the window, eyes murky from the mottled glaze of the glass. Dressed in black, she's a stark contrast to the red and white candy-stripe and gummy bear bright coloured exterior of her house. So inviting—like a carnival funhouse and candy shop—it's hard not to try one little gingerbread-looking corner.

The old lady smiles, and her face splits and ripples, distorted by the dappled glass. A small boy is in front of her, licking the window. She laughs and takes him by the hand.

"Come along, Hansel," she cackles. "It's time for my dinner."

Dark Hands
by Blakewood Grey

Pale hands plunge. The bowl is warm, its contents dark—not black, not entirely red—yet it lies red upon the skin. A thin paint, that trickles, irritating into madness at the elbows.

Red hands withdraw. They aren't empty, nor pale, nor innocent. Fists close, encircled by that most vibrant gore – an artwork of life, etched from fleshy canvas. A testament to death; an epitaph of hunger.

That fragile, fleeting thing.

He craves. To take it; own it; command it. The lapping blood before him is but a taste. A mere suggestion of the still-beating heart clasped in his fist.

Together Forever
by Denys Breuse

Wailing, I collapse to my knees against the gravestone, batting away consoling hands.

The mourners leave me to my grief.

At last I'm alone.

I fall onto my back in the dirt…and laugh at the darkening sky. *No one suspects!*

"I did it," I yell. The perfect crime!

But then the earth moves beneath me. A mud-caked hand reaches from consecrated depths, an arm wraps around my neck in a final embrace.

My last breath escapes.

I'm pulled below the surface, a mound of freshly dug soil the only evidence I was ever there.

He whispers, "You did it."

Youthful Glow
by Jonni Gore

His younger lover used to sneer at Grey when he was drunk. "You look good…for your age."

Grey held no illusions about the young man's interest, but it still stung.

He hadn't endured the ridicule of younger men for over a decade.

* * *

Grey knocked firmly and waited. The door opened to reveal a man of fading beauty—and unfaded arrogance.

He blinked. "Grey?"

"May I come in?"

He invited Grey in. "You look good!"

Grey seized the man, snarling, "For my age?"

His fangs plunged deep before the man could answer, syphoning every last drop of his youthful glow.

The Rescue
by Elle Cameron

Until the rescue and the shocking news reports, she was a prisoner. Her feet only knew concrete. Her tongue only knew vile, stale things.

In the hospital, there were outbursts: she pulled a scrap of scalp from a nurse's head.

I gave her a bedroom. Clothes. Toys. A squashy stuffed rabbit.

But, drawn to the dark and the cold, she claimed the basement.

One morning I found the squashy rabbit hanging by a noose, blood dripping from its floppy ear.

Horror overwhelmed me. Where had the blood come from? Then I understood—she didn't need to be rescued. I did.

John Doe
by K.W. Reeds

It's dark and cold when I wake.

I turn my head. My vision clears, and the glazed-over, hollowed-out eyes of a girl stare back at me, her ghastly, bloody maw open in a long-dead scream.

I scream too—it's deadened in the confines of the fridge, so no one hears.

I hear far-off voices, dull whispers, and then the door opens. I slide out of the cold, closing my eyes to the sudden blinding light.

My heart falters, stops forever.

As my world fades to black, I hear, "This one's a John Doe—"

But then their scent awakens the Zee.

The Exe's Revenge
by Damon Brodie

Sophie screamed as Jordan stepped off the platform.

His body was pulled for a few meters, leaving a smear of blood on the concrete, before disappearing under the wheels of the train.

She sank to the ground, still howling, and a consoling arm moved across her shoulders. "Come on, darl. Let's get you away from here."

She allowed herself to be led to a bench and she sobbed in a stranger's lap. "This was our first date!" she cried. "I don't understand!"

* * *

Two smiling faces look back at Amy from Sophie's profile as a skewered doll drops from her lap.

Housebound
by Jameson Grey

Often when leaving the house, Cynthia locked her husband in the cupboard under the stairs.

He liked it dark—said his mind ran wild in there—and Cynthia loved the control it gave her. Her husband had a wandering eye and this way she knew where he was.

Always. *Almost* always. Until her husband ruined it with yet another affair.

Cynthia confronted him—he said he'd leave her for this one—so the next time she went out, she invited his mistress home.

At least now Cynthia knows where both of them are bound.

In her cupboard. Under the stairs.

OK, Boomer
by Lance Dale

He emerged from the lake brandishing his machete. It had been thirty years since the Summer Camp Massacre. Seven camp counsellors killed. The lone survivor was the only one not taking drugs or having sex. This was the code. He admired his blade. It was ready.

When he reached the camp, all the counsellors were sitting in a circle staring at screens. No sex. No drugs. No murder. Disappointment overwhelmed him.

"What is the matter with you!? You're supposed to be engaging in debauchery!" he shouted.

"Okay, Boomer." they replied.

This was the start of the second Summer Camp Massacre.

Weep
by Dominique Bourdon

Here I sit upon on my charge's final resting place; a stone effigy, weeping tears for this child, for his suffering. This is my eternal fate; for my failures will haunt me for eternity and I shall cry silently forever in sadness and desolation.

But I wait.

For when *he* comes—and he *will* come—revenge will be mine. The father's eyes will gaze upon me and I shall torment his soul for the suffering he inflicted; he will writhe in my anger, suffocate in my hatred, fester in my rage.

And if he looks away, I will devour him.

Night Maere
by Jaycee Durand

Open your eyes. Observe your fate.

Petrified into stillness, my muscles quiver in vain. God, help me, what crushes my chest so? I barely push any breath past my lips. An oppressive presence smothers my very being.

W-who's there? Am I dreaming?

Open your eyes.

My eyelashes flutter against the gloom, akin to the flapping wings of a trapped bird. I don't want to see. It's just a dream...

Talons pierce my flesh.

...can't be real. Leaden eyelids rise—a rictus grin goads me.

Her whisper rasps against my ears as she settles to feed.

The Night Hag has come.

Dating My Daughter
by J.D. Frain

Only a few remaining in this one-road town.

GinnySue was a spry thirteen first time she brought one home.

Settin' round the burn barrel, GinnySue holdin' Aiden's hand, me cleaning my Remington. "Tell one a your stories, Daddy," she begs.

Picked the one about the drifter come up from Oklahoma. One who whined account I wouldn't let him date GinnySue till she's eighteen. Wasn't in GinnySue's league besides.

"He's still waiting." I wink, pointing my Remington at Aiden's shoes. "Right 'neath where you're settin'."

Aiden tripped, he run off so fast.

Saturday, GinnySue brings home the Williams boy, I'm done.

The Enemy Within
by Dawn Knox

The parasitic worm hatches in the moist, dark environment of the animal's intestines; unseeing and unthinking, but voraciously hungry.

With hooks embedded in the host's gut, it secretes digestive enzymes which break down cells, and it greedily ingests the resultant biological mush. The greater the mess of liquefied cells, the larger it grows.

Initially, the host is unaware of the worm dissolving its internal organs. But eventually, everything will rupture, releasing blood and putrescent tissue. Soon, the pulped insides will seep out of the animal through all orifices, and with it, the engorged parasite ready to find another unsuspecting host.

The Birthday Collection
by Margarida Brei

My latest boyfriend thought the wooden urn on the mantelpiece held a family member's ashes.

Fool!

He was shocked to see so many. Several in every single room and always placed effectively; front and centre.

I was a braggart about those cinerary urns.

My boyfriend prattled on about the beautiful workmanship and ornate carvings. Noticing the date—27th March 2019—on one urn, he commented that it was my last birthday, and wasn't today my birthday? I nodded, adding that every urn was dated 27th March but a different year as I sank my teeth into his tasty tender tissue.

The Maddening Sound
by Alec Thompson

Richard looks at himself in the mirror. The maddening sound drones away in his brain. Twenty years, driving him mad—and only getting worse.

On the counter, a drill with a one-eighth bit. He's done the measuring. The perfect size to penetrate and erase the apparatus.

It's in his ear and he's pulling the trigger and there's not the carnage he'd envisioned. He does the second one, quick, runnels of blood down his neck. Then the drill's off, and everything's still. In the mirror, his mouth drops open in a silent scream, as all he can hear is the tinnitus.

The Visitor
by Birgit K. Gaiser

During his brief spells of consciousness, pain travelled across his body like ants crawling through his veins, like rats nibbling on his exposed skin.

He had begged and threatened, had dragged sharp rocks over his wrists, again and again. After the beatings, the starvation, the filth, his captors were still keeping him alive for more.

He heard footsteps. Suddenly, after weeks of darkness, blinding torchlight assaulted his senses.

His eyes adjusted, focussed on the hand holding the torch. A familiar hand, missing two fingers.

Next, her other hand came into view, holding a knife. His knife.

"Hi, honey," she said

Unexpected
by Karen Thrower

I leaned against my car, annoyed that it died on the side of a country road. The heat of the day was still sizzling off the pavement, even though the sun had been down for an hour. I pulled my phone out to call AAA, but there was no signal. *Of course.*

Bright lights made me squint. I tried to shield my eyes, but it was everywhere. When my eyes adjusted, I saw the sky was filled with millions of flying discs, spinning silently.

I looked up as a beam engulfed me, and I started floating up towards the ship.

Loves Lost
by Gene Lee

It's hard sometimes; to remember my hidden place, my refuge from this cruel world, the space that always gave me comfort.

The long forgotten garden with its surrounding trees standing like sentries, guarding the pond with its calming, lapping waters comes back to me in my dreams.

Those cool shadows where I could lie and watch the dying of the sun, feel its waning warmth and no one knew I was there.

And then, by the light of the ethereal moon, I dug my children's last resting place, and washed their sticky blood from my skin in the chilly pool.

An Unforgettable Night
by Adrian David

"Tonight's gonna be epic." She flashed a seductive smile, her deep golden eyes glowing under the starlit sky. Her chalk-pale fingers unbuttoned his shirt.

Their eyes locked, so did their lips. She slowly moved to his neck, planting featherlight kisses. Getting turned on by her every move, he closed his eyes in pleasure, waiting for her to make love.

Suddenly, her fangs pierced his neck. He shrieked, as she drained him of blood. Smacking her scarlet lips, she relished the flavour of AB negative.

His lifeless body fell with a thud. Alas, yet another hunk succumbed to the vampire's bloodthirst.

A Demon's Snack
by Radar DeBoard

His thumb pushed the malleable material towards the opposite side of the socket. This gave just enough room for his index finger to slip in and get some traction underneath. Then it only took a few gentle tugs to pluck it from its hole.

Bifrons smiled as he carefully brought the orb out for inspection. With careful fingers, and a quick snip just below the eye, he cleanly severed all the nerves.

Bifrons brought it up to his lips and took a bite. He just couldn't resist a good eye. After all, it was his favourite part of the human.

Due to a Combination of Faulty Genes
by Christopher T. Dabrowski
translated by Julia Mraczny

He was ugly. There was no way to hide it. And it didn't help that some women love ugly men.

Lonely, bitter, with self-hatred bubbling under his skin, he stood in front of the mirror, panting with rage at Mother Nature and the unfortunate combination of genes...

Suddenly the mirror exploded, showering him with razor-sharp pieces of glass, hurting him.

* * *

The ugly being on the other side of the mirror experienced the same. Furious, he launched a right hook, aiming straight at his face in the mirror.

The glass shattered the reflection and fell to the floor with a clatter.

Stains
by Robert Balentine Jr.

"Mommy, can you wash my baby doll? Tommy messed her dress."

I throw her rag doll into the washing machine without looking and press start. Everything has a bewildering pale pink sheen when I go to put it in the dryer and I reach for my special detergent, the one with "Active Oxygen Bleaching!" that I reserve for toddler-sized messes.

"Mommy, can you wash my shirt, too?"

Crimson splashes decorate her white cotton T-shirt. The smell of iron fills my nose.

I look down at my blood-spattered child and the sewing scissors in her hands.

"Lucy, where is your brother?"

Submission
by Munday Locke

They queue.

With gaunt faces and bloodshot eyes, weary feet trudge slowly. The line snakes down the hill, back and forth between the hellfires, all eyes on the stooped shoulders in front. Silence, but for quiet groans.

He watches.

Three crimson eyes glow eerily in the dark; all that can be seen of the black Hellhare as he waits in the shadows.

Trembling hands lift their offerings to the altar, reverently placing it upon the last. Some even shed a single tear.

His soul aches.

For he knows he is the maker of dreams, but also the breaker of hearts.

Dear Slavic Santa
by Jaden Apollo

A crimson plash seeped out from 'neath the prettily wrapped box as Yekaterina descended the stairs, eyes wide and sparkling in the dancing lights of the tree.

She'd been woken by a noise downstairs and had tiptoed to her parents' door to peek in before investigating—still forms made no sounds.

She ripped open the gift and two still-warm, still beating hearts fell out into her lap. She gasped, knowing instantly they belonged to her parents.

Startled by a noise at the window, she looked up. Ded Moroz winked at her before disappearing.

She knew then he'd received her letter…

Hey Beautiful, Dance with Me
by A.H. Syme

You can do it. Yes, you can.

Now, slowly expose your neck. Fear makes your jugular vein pulse, swell—purple and juicy—and the more you fight my hypnotic suggestions and resist, the more pain you'll feel.

What? You hate me? I'm no longer sexy. Foolish girl. You were enthralled by me before. Remember dancing, when you stuck your tongue down my throat? Did you not get just a hint of decay? Don't you know I am beyond erotic, beyond flesh?

I'm death's shame.

I fabricate life.

Ah, yes. Do cry—it adds a tang of salt to my sauce.

Stone Harvest
by Woodrow Fleer

The grey cloud seeps into the room
Mote by mote it gathers above the bed
Where the man lies dying
Motes congeal
Torso of a lion
Wings of a bat
A fanged half-human face
Gaining weight, descending

The old and evil fight
Against the dying of the light
The beast presses down
Strain grows with every breath
A final gasp
The last breath exits
The soul with it
The beast opens its maw and inhales

Wings flair, it dissipates

Motes scatter and escape outside

The cloud floats away

It returns home to solidify

A gargoyle guard on the Cathedral roof

The Number of a Man
by Maggie D. Brace

"The number of a man is important. I always want to know what sort of man I'm dealing with." That's what she had tantalised me with before she sweetly smiled and turned away.

Little did she suspect; my number was six hundred three score and six.

Musing, I followed her progress through the bar, simpering up to men, whispering in their ear, then flashing that same saccharine smile and slinking away.

I followed her home that night.

Pulling up my sleeve, I slowly and painfully carved my sacred number. Warm, salty droplets caressed my fingers. She would remember me forever.

The Mask
by Stuart Conover

Scotty lay down at the banks of the shore, the mask before him.

When had he been able to last remove it? Days? Weeks? Months? Memories blended together.

Blood splattered the mask. He could still smell it.

Taste it.

Scotty's stomach emptied. He refused to acknowledge what he threw up.

What, or who, the mask had made him eat.

Blood permeated the air.

Scotty looked back. The husks of three corpses lay there. Drained, half eaten, rotting.

He backed away, hands touching the mask.

He wanted to forget it all.

He could.

Scotty just had to put it back on.

The Tooth Fairy's Apprentice
by Harold Hoss

I never intended to lie to my son—I wanted him to have a normal childhood. I hid the bills, the past due notices, and signs of our money problems.

And, although money was tight, I put a shiny silver dollar under his pillow when he lost his first tooth, feigning surprise when he showed me his treasure the next morning.

But I didn't have to act surprised a month later when, lifting his pillow, he revealed a small pile of teeth, still slick with blood and undeniably human. "Now we can pay the bills, Daddy. Just wait. You'll see."

Dental Work
by Gus Wood

Verne laughed in the mirror at his new teeth. Polished and slick as the real things never were, they beamed out his mouth like a slice of moonlight.

He could eat like he wanted again. He could chew again. It was good news for Verne. "Best thing since hitchhiking," he'd say.

But, with Verne's car parked outside the office, with Verne's taillights following him home, and the way Verne ran his tongue across his teeth, when the dentist's sweet family ran up to greet him, it would be very bad news for the man who'd given Verne his bite back.

Livestock
by R.J. Meldrum

"Those five," said Stan to the ranch hands.

Hank, standing beside him at the fence, stared out at the pen. He was new, two weeks into the job. The sight still amazed him.

"I can't believe it. The plague was meant to have died out before I was born."

"It did, but we kept two as breed stock."

"And the customers don't know?"

"It's marketed as dry-aged beef."

"Where do you get them?"

"Hikers, campers, hitchhikers. Once they're here, we infect them. Six weeks later the flesh is aged to perfection."

Hank stared out at the milling zombies.

"Just amazing."

Complexion
by Frances Lu-Pai Ippolito

Xiao-Li dabbed foundation over her cheeks, choosing a golden shade. Angling her chin, she blended the liquid into skin stretched across her jawbone, ignoring the red smears of mingled blood seeping out a creased flap.

"Damn!" she yelled, hurling the sponge at the mirror. This simply wasn't the right colour, blend, or face. Slipping a fingernail under the crease, she peeled off the skin and tossed it into a bin.

Nearby, body-sized bags whimpered and screamed.

Gingerly touching her exposed muscles and wet veins, Xiao-Li grinned, knife in hand. At least she had a couple of free samples to try.

Linguistic Conservation
by Bernardo Villela

Before me lies another severed tongue. A cruel operation for a noble end: preserving idioms that might die with their speakers. Until the dead rise and speak, my magic is the only way to save them.

As with many collectors, I have become obsessed—always wanting a fast track to learn new languages.

Today I will meet with another potential successor, someone who might be an apprentice and my partner. In my home there are a bounty tongues in many lockboxes yearning to speak anew, and many more to acquire.

Cleaning off my knife, I see my newest donor waking.

The Concrete Tomb
by Lynne Phillips

The face of a man I don't know is hard against mine, his last breath long gone. It's been three days since the earthquake.

My body is trapped under the rubble; I can't move my arms or legs. I shallow breathe, rationing the small pocket of air.

The rescue teams and sniffer dogs, searching for signs of life are close, I can hear them. I moisten my lips, my voice pleading for help, but it's lost, absorbed by my concrete tomb. The voices recede and I realise they have moved on. The dozers move in and the concrete shifts again.

Throb
by Alyanna Poe

He reached through my back, tickling my spine with a brush of his hand. His fingers gently wrapped around my still beating heart, and he plucked it free without a word.

I gasped as he took it, turning to face him.

"Such a fine specimen," he said, looking over my heart. It pulsed in his hand, slowing as it died. He put it to his lips and took a big bite.

He smiled at me as he chewed, blood dripping down his chin and onto his shirt.

I curled my lip, returning the smile.

Too bad my fruit was poisonous.

He Came
by Lauren Winter

Candlelight danced in the wind, giving life to the shadows in the trees. Chimes from the femurs strung between the trees created hollow tones that floated through the forest; a tranquil melody accented by the rustling of the trees.

Her heart fluttered. Taking a knife to her wrists, she danced, letting the blood flow down her arm and drip from her fingertips. Drums beat in the distance as she began to hum the ancient call.

A figure walked froward from the shadows, eyes burning red and antlers reaching to the sky.

"My prince," she whispered, and sank into his arms.

Lucky Devil
by Tracy Davidson

Sharp claws cut slivers of soft flesh. Humans taste better served rare, while pounding hearts still beat, blood seasoned with adrenalin. The best hosts can keep meat alive for hours.

But my guests are too hungry to wait. And my new bride hungers for more than food.

She makes the deep cut, turning her white dress scarlet.

The meat voices one final scream. It dies, watching my beloved gorging on its guts.

Beautiful.

We consummate on a bed of bowel and bones. Demon seed passes between us. It will grow and grow until it kills me.

I'm a lucky devil.

Grinning Teeth
by Sean M. Palfrey

Every night they're there. Shining in the darkness. Puncturing the gloom, sharp and malevolent. They never move though...never make a sound. No growls, no gnashing. They just grin at me with an impish knowing about them.

There's no other shape. No eyes. No breath in the cold winter air. Just teeth. Grinning at me from the shadows at the foot of my bed. Daring me to get up and turn on the light. Instead, I pull the sheets around me tighter until the dawn light banishes them for another day.

No teeth. Just pools of saliva on the floor.

In Their Wake
by Dorian J. Sinnott

It was just before October when the vultures came. The dreary cemetery at the top of the hill hardly saw life, and their coming was almost a relief. I spent the early evenings watching them in their wake, perched upon gravestones and in old trees—wings wide in a haunting dance. Yet, while I found their presence comforting, I began to feel as though eyes were always watching me every time I left home. Every day at dusk, from outside my window. From the trees. There are more of them than before—near fresh, overturned graves. Plucking flesh from bone.

Fetish
by Destiny Eve Pifer

Glenda awoke, dazed and shivering, to find herself tied to a chair in a strange, red room.

How had she come to be there? She couldn't remember.

To clear the fog, she shook her head. "Think Glenda!"

After her blind date had said those repugnant words about lusting after her feet, she'd stood up to leave. Everything after that was a blank.

Sighing, she looked down with bleary-eyed regret at her open-toed shoes, but found it difficult to focus.

After some squinting, she was rewarded with the realisation that the red carpeting was blood and that her feet were missing.

Snow Day
by Sam Lesek

"My dad says that we shouldn't be out in the cold," Tom said to the other boy. "He had a friend who disappeared in a blizzard."

Tom noticed the boy's strange clothes and soot-coloured fingertips.

"Are you cold?"

The boy nodded. Tom passed him his knitted mittens. They waited along the snowy, forested road.

"That's my dad's van." Tom pointed towards the oncoming vehicle. He felt a chill when he saw the shock in his father's face as the van slowed to a halt.

The strange boy waved. Tom looked over to see his blue lips stretching into a smile.

Daddy's Girl
by Robyn Fraser

When things got tough, she still liked to hold her father's hand.

Even though she was all grown up now, with a job and a nice house and everything.

When life felt too big for her, when she was overwhelmed and couldn't cope, having his big, work-gnarled hand in hers made her feel instantly better.

He'd screamed when she'd taken it, but not for long.

When things got tough, she still liked to hold her father's hand.

It reminded her that she was in control. *She* would decide how her life went. *She* would decide what touched her, and where.

Go into STEM
by N.S. Reiss

Programming all the rage, money and security,

Genetic engineering nucleobase code

Quaternary Theory makes AI old history.

Brain bootcamp graduate of cybernetics course load,

My employment began at the pet design agency.

Clients ignore gene cocktail risks, lining up to

Buy companions off shelves like nutritional ghee.

Deformed runts exist, life ain't a perfect brew,

Adolescent *sapiens* rebel and disagree,

Cute no longer when personality flourishes.

Defective bipeds that return to the pound,

They don't get second chances,

To dust they are ground.

Promotions slide by, days turn to years unknowingly.

I love my job

And the food is free.

Strawberry Jam
by Warren Benedetto

I slipped through the cellar window and into the abandoned house. The doctor who owned the place had allegedly performed illegal abortions in the basement.

This basement.

My flashlight illuminated a shelf of Mason jars, each labelled as "StrawBerry Jam." Stefan said they were filled with the liquified remains of aborted babies. He dared me to steal one.

I held a jar up to the light. Something inside bumped against the glass. I screamed.

I left without the jar.

I never told anyone what I'd seen.

But when I close my eyes, I can still see the tiny hand inside.

The Return of the Butcher
by David Bowmore

Janet wakes. Through a pink haze, she sees skinless limbs dangling from meat hooks—presumably the remains of her husband.

A grinding sound in the next room stops, and the butcher returns, humming a light tune.

"Ah, good. You're awake," she says. "I've finished mincing. And I'm boiling his head and feet to sell as brawn. I hope your liver is in better condition than his."

Mira presses a razor-sharp knife to Janet's throat.

"Why are you doing this, Mira?" Janet asks, voice all of a tremor.

Mira bends and kisses Janet's bloody lips, and then says, "I really don't know."

Shockingly Real
by Gabriella Balcom

Seeing the body on the platter, Kenny's eyes widened. An axe protruded from the head, which was split open. It looked shockingly real—the brain and blood. A metallic tang hung in the air.

A green ooze-covered creature sliced the brain, while a two-headed werewolf cut chunks from the body.

Kenny bit into one, chuckling when red liquid squirted out. Somebody had gone all-out for this Halloween party.

Then he noticed the guests' glowing eyes. Realising the truth, he panicked and fled.

Monsters caught Kenny quickly. Ignoring his screams, they ripped him apart, cramming handfuls of flesh into their mouths.

The Midnight Beast
by Deni Oiticica

Only Danny can stop the beast.

Stalking the scent of perfume, the creature crawls up a fire escape and slithers through a cracked window.

"No! Never again!"

Danny hurries, close in pursuit. Straining against the window is useless—it won't budge.

"Run! Hide!" he yells, banging on the window.

She cries and screams inside her room, her eyes wide with terror.

The demon leers, taunting Danny from inside.

Crowbar steel smashes frosty glass, clearing his path. He resists the demon with all his might. Yet never enough.

As Danny swings, wrecks, and ruins, his face is sprayed red... Sticky...

Again...

Cheese
by Brooke Percy

A car rounded the sharp bend in the road too quickly and spun out. The crunch of metal as it flipped caught the attention of a man in a nearby farmhouse. He ran towards the wreck; found a woman in the driver's seat. She blinked blood from her eyes as he approached her shattered window. A gash marred her face, and a large piece of glass pierced her abdomen.

"Help," she pleaded. The man pulled his phone from his pocket…and opened the camera app. He filmed until the light left the woman's eyes; smiled. Another video for his collection.

Congregation
by Henry Myllylä

Nine moons came to their feverish end at a desolate cove, where Mathilda, now wailing in pain, delivers her baby into Miriam's bloodied hands by a bonfire.

As Miriam cuts the umbilical cord with her rusted scissors, it's quiet. Way too quiet, so Miriam gives the lifeless, gory lump a shake. Then she casts it into the raging flames.

"No, no..." Mathilda pleads, seeing the Horned One in their presence displeased.

Miriam kneels down by Mathilda's side. She grasps Mathilda's throat and holds the scissors up high. Mathilda's womb had failed their congregation, but her heart has still its use.

The Great One
by Sophie Wagner

The green flames circled Henry, trapping him. Or rather, what was left of Henry.

As the chanting of his captors grew in volume, more of his skin began to rot and fall off his body, exposing bones that continued to snap and grow back at funny angles.

Henry screamed in agony as horns broke through his scalp, spilling black blood down his face. Yet when the blood fell into his eyes, it did not matter. He could no longer feel anything. He wasn't even Henry anymore.

"We welcome you, Great One!" the ringleader yelled. "Bow to the Prince of Hell!

The Offering
by S.A. McKenzie

Through many winters I have waited in these mountains, curled around my hunger in the dark. My priests would bring the sacrifices up the long stone staircase to offer themselves to me, their arms raised in worship.

Then the pale strangers from across the sea brought sickness to this land, and now my priests are no more.

* * *

New voices outside my temple speak an unfamiliar tongue.

"You were right, Chad, it was worth the climb!"

"Stand there, Tina. Arms up! Now, smile!"

The girl's eyes widen. Her mouth opens in a silent scream as I rise. The offering is accepted.

Simplification
by B.T. Petro

The cover of the book on my wife's nightstand explained her actions over the past few days. *Declutter to Simplify Your Life* had the tagline: "If it doesn't bring you joy, get rid of it."

Two days ago, she sold the golf clubs that I bought her. They'd sat unused for several years. They brought her no joy.

Yesterday, she took the pottery we bought on our honeymoon to the curb. Many pieces were broken. They brought her no joy.

This morning, there's the body on our bedroom floor. It may have been the infidelity. I brought her no joy.

The Picnic
by April Yates

They won't allow the doll to come home with us.

"Broken." "Dirty." "Why do you want it when you've plenty of toys at home?" "Things that are found in the woods should stay there."

They weren't watching their daughter when she wondered into the undergrowth and found me; the switch done in the time it took them to unpack their picnic.

I ate ravenously, never having tasted actual food before; my plastic lips could never part for it.

I'd like my old body for sentimental reasons but drop it on their command.

Perhaps, someday, another little girl will find it.

Apartment 251
by Brian Rosenberger

They were at it again. Damn neighbours creating a racket at this ungodly hour. The sheer nerve of them. Roy told his wife, Loretta, to stay put. He'd handle things. Not the police. Not the landlord.

The noise was worse than a cat in heat. Were they butchering some cow in sacrifice? Roy pounded on the door, causing it to open. Turns out it wasn't a cow but Johnson, the tenant in Apartment 248. He was another odd bird. Night owl.

Nude and hanging from the ceiling, Johnson smiled. "Welcome to the party."

The other partygoers showed Roy their knives.

Mourning Son
by Kate Lowe

I jerk from the clutch of a feverish dream, disturbed by a sound like the tearing of paper. Sweat-slicked, panting, bound in a tangle of bedsheets, I'm rigid. The bedroom, tomblike, is shrouded in darkness as thick and black as old blood.

The noise comes again, not the rending of paper but the *scritch* of brittle nails against age-worn oak as the thing beneath the bed claws its way into the open. My heart bangs hard against my ribcage, a condemned prisoner of its foolhardy host.

Ma told me she'd come back for me.

I guess she kept her promise.

Just Hanging Out
by Amanda Evans

It hung, twirling from its lucky paw, the hind right. It dripped blood on the foliage and wheezed. I couldn't kill it, and it was too far gone to save. I smoked a joint and got high watching it die.

Morbid curiosity made me poke it, scattering drops of copper-scented crimson, destroying the pattern of nature's tiny lake.

Am I a monster? I wondered, feeling the cool fur brush my hand on the return swing, then giggled. That thought was way too grand for me right now.

Patting the dead thing once more, I continued travelling through the silent woods.

Quench
by Darke Blud

I hear footsteps!

My heart pounds like the Slipnot drummer, sweat tickles my forehead. I hold my breath, trying to figure out where they're coming from, how close they are. My eyes dart around deserted streets.

Sidestepping into an alley, I wait for the footfalls to pass by.

Teetering on stilettos, she never even had chance to let out a cry. My hand covers her mouth, my arm encircles her neck, and I drag her into the shadows.

The blade slices through her pulse as Joey Jordison's encore plays in my heart. Leaving clues, I lick crimson from her throat.

Graveyard
by B.J. Thrower

The Moon was a vast, pitiless cemetery. Julian's crew discovered it an hour ago from the underground-imaging probes. The dead displayed on her screens: Hulking alien skeletons, each with unique horns protruding from massive skulls. Delicate "birds" attached to cartilage-strings leading parades of winged offspring. Curled in death was an ape-like beast with overlong arms and fangs.

And human remains too; a woman, bony fingers clutching an unborn foetus's skeleton, or men carrying children. Millions, billions buried in lunar basalts.

Adisa's finger, pointing over Julian's shoulder at the monitor. "What *is* it?"

"A burial ground. The end of colonisation."

The Dark Lord's Cure
by Dawn DeBraal

Flaming torches. The smell of disease and sickness. Young and old jostling in close quarters. They chant, demanding his blood.

"Save us." But the Dark Lord can't help them all. Nervously, his eyes flick to the bell tower clock—he can only control them a little longer. Relieved, he hears the distant rumble.

"My people, you have your cure—my blood is yours," he announced. Rejoicing cries. Mothers weep in relief.

"*He has heard our cries.*"

The sound of joyous celebration rises, reverberating through the town square, masking the sound of his tanks.

His army will cure the sick forever.

The Game
by Andrew McDonald

A joke became a dare, then a game.

For hours they drove, looking for a contestant.

Nearing 4 a.m. they saw him—alone, thumb extended.

Pulling over, the driver jumped out, popped the trunk and grabbed a shotgun.

He ordered the contestant to his knees; he refused. Stepping closer, the driver yelled again.

The passengers shouted protests, momentarily distracting the driver.

Grabbing the gun, the contestant dropped him with a right-handed punch. The 12 gauge splattered the driver's brains over the road.

He ordered the passengers out, gesturing to the woods with the gun. "One minute."

They scrambled.

His game.

Darkness
by Kateri Tough

Melinda lurched awake. Her black hair was plastered to her sweaty forehead, her eyes wide open, as if it would help her see in the pitch-black bedroom.

Melinda stumbled out of bed, heart beating hard and fast. It was so dark, she had to feel her way down the hall towards her mother's bedroom. The only sounds were the floor creaking underfoot and her own laboured breathing.

She opened the door and whispered, "Mama!" There was a pause, then a bloodcurdling scream.

"Your eyes!" Melinda's mother cried. Melinda moved her hands to her face. All she felt were empty sockets.

Dinner
by Kimberly Rei

Shadows caught the hooks lining the walls, hinting at a glistening sheen. The dim bulb wavered too much to allow for any sort of focus, but my eyes followed the swaying even as primal memory demanded my attention. There was something familiar about all this.

The scent of rancid blood. A slow drip. Why couldn't I remember? How had I arrived here?

Rustling drew my gaze. A body squirmed, waking up and screaming as the hook further ripped open their chest.

My mouth watered and I licked my teeth. I knew who I was. Where I was.

I was home.

Even in the Dark
by S. Jade Path

Tears welling, a fourth arrow pierced her deeply. She'd escaped but lost track of when. Chittering laughter chased her.

The exit in sight; she refused to be taken.

She dragged herself through the gates.

A fifth arrow pierced, and she froze where she'd begun, her scream echoing across the gunmetal plane.

* * *

A skittering drew her gaze, memories of pain dissipating. An ear turned her way; the hare's past written in scars.

Carefully she reached out.

Nose twitching furiously, it placed its paw gently and hopped into her lap.

A moment of mutual comfort in an otherwise cruel and hollow world.

Lover of the Lost
by Hari Navarro

He collects bloated things that hook in swirling currents within the distributary channel that stagnates behind the wall at the end of his garden.

Dripping sacks of discarded pets are lugged into his redbrick basement, but today a young woman lies upon the slab. He kisses eyelids and lips eaten away, and fearlessly purrs as he runs his scalpel through the puffy wax of her peeling and swollen abdomen.

He sways, lost in a strange type of sweat, until an eel oozes out of the opening in a gush of necrotic fluid and costs him the end of his tongue.

Incubator
by Bill Hughes

Unseen, it captured him from behind. The chill of its limbs—arms? tentacles?—blistered his skin, despite his wetsuit. He stopped screaming to save air as they rocketed downward. Rough spines pierced his back, burrowing through skin and muscle and finding, with agonizing precision, their places. When his tank emptied, he didn't suffocate; the spikes penetrating his lungs supplied oxygen. A trio of alien rhythms maintained circulation after his heart stopped.

He began to shriek when the slick tendril pressed its way between his thighs, and he continued shrieking while the ovipositor pumped his rectum full of small, gelid eggs.

Played Out
by Jen Mierisch

"A talented young pianist," they called Darien.

I had other names for him.

The theatre was as hushed as a funeral. Seated in the last row, I waited, my jewels glittering like eyes in the darkness. I'd dressed for the occasion.

His hands tore through Morel's *Étude de Sonorité No. 2*, heading for that highest C. When its hammer tapped that string, it would trip the wire I'd placed there. And then, either he'd never use those cheating hands again, or he'd be blown straight to hell where he belonged.

Watching, I shed a single tear for the baby grand.

Desolation
by S.J. Crowe

I awake to find myself in a graveyard. This is beyond bizarre!

Tombstones—all with my name carved upon them with utmost care. I stare in awe at the sight before me. I am sure, as if fact, my eyes are deceiving me.

Ambling my way onwards, the clouds are growing darker, and all I see around me is blood—all the graves are covered in the crimson of the living.

That moment, a thought strikes me. As life's vital liquid still appears fresh, I surmise it can only be from a recent corpse.

My path is blocked.

Death awaits.

Tender and Bittersweet
by Miriam H. Harrison

When she held his head to the starlight, she could almost see the old gleam in his eyes. In that gleam were the memories, tender and bittersweet. It had taken time to draw him out, draw him close. He had been hurt before, he had said. "It won't be like that," she had said.

And it wasn't. When her hunger came, she made sure it was painless for him. She had given him her word, and he gave her the memories, gave her everything.

She left his head behind, there with his bones, and went in search of fresh memories.

Semi-Automatic
by James Flanagan

An ancient automaton. I wind it up. Its turban sits askew upon its partial head. An eye dangles.

Rusted hands meet and part as if shuffling cards. It places the imaginary deck on the table and reveals an invisible card. The voice creaks.

"You will...kill."

My skin tingles, I try to dismiss it—as mindless repetition—but for the mantra stencilled on the automaton's chest. "No escaping destiny."

Old wounds open up and spill my trauma. Penetrated, violated, ignored at the police station.

Fate then. "But how?" I reach for the crank. The automaton grins and winds itself instead.

On the Mattress
by Conrad Gardner

Your body. Your tight, pale body. It's lying there, on the canvas of my bed.

We're naked. Both of us. Your nipples are hard. I'm hard. As I run my hands around you, clutching your back, holding you close, your arm flops over, strokes my ass. Cheeky. I move it back where it's meant to be, on my hip.

You're cold to the touch. It's funny. In the coffin, you were warmer. Was it the ground? I'll never know. But we're back together, like we should be.

After I finish, we're spooning again, nuzzling.

We're hugging and kissing, like before.

The Gallows Dancers
by Leanbh Pearson

He liked to see the hangman work, the sound of the rope stretching and groaning. He would watch the feet tap, tap, tapping in the air, dancers swinging to a music only they could hear. How he would watch their faces, enraptured, while skin darkened to blue, then purple, swollen faces like over-ripe fruit after harvest. When blackened tongues protruded from swollen lips in one last mocking of the crowd, he knew the dance was at its end.

But he would pray, eyes fixed on the hanging tree. *Oh hangman, let the gallows dancers spin for me in another dirge?*

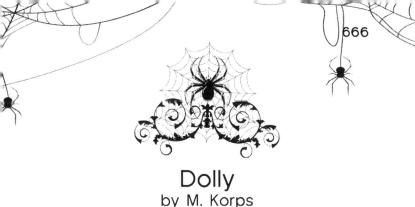

Dolly
by M. Korps

It was an exact replica of her, curly hair and all, capturing the glimmer of her hazel eyes and the essence of her smile. Overjoyed, he caressed the miniature version of his wife in his hands.

"Twist its head," she said.

He did.

To his horror, her neck snapped. Shards of vertebrae burst through her throat as blood began gushing down her neck.

He stumbled to her, squeezing her growingly cold body in his arms, watching her slowly choke to silence. A piece of parchment slipped out her pocket.

I didn't have the courage to do it myself... I'm sorry.

Barbed Comment
by Doug Jacquier

On display, at a party given by a woman artist, was a stuffed cushion representing a stylised vagina, complete with pubic hair fashioned from steel wool. Male guests were encouraged to insert their fingers into the 'vagina' to demonstrate their lack of fear. I dutifully did so, then yelped in pain as my hand met the barbed wire interior. Every woman there laughed. Underneath the 'sculpture' was a hall stand with disinfectant and Band-Aids. I reached for them, but the artist whispered fiercely in my ear that these were ironic inclusions in the piece and pointed me to the bathroom.

Angel Lust
by River South

The succubus passes the mirror, glances her own nakedness. Cool hands stroke pert breasts, hard nipples.

Teeth tease full red lips; she's *hungry*.

She pads—bare feet, light steps, dark curls caressing skin—to the bed. Tangled sheets drape him, filtered moonlight illuminates olive skin.

She sees he's…*ready*.

She presses a kiss against his lips. Legs part, she straddles him—he doesn't stir. She sinks slowly, eyes closed, breath held, lost in the fullness as her aching coldness envelopes his…

…his…

…his coldness…

Realisation; post-death priapism… Her eyes pop open—another COVID victim lies stiff between her thighs.

Succulent
by Alison Waddy

"The desert knows how to drink blood," the hooded man says, as fat drops of it well from my bound wrists and fall into the dust.

"And it knows," he continues, nudging at a long-spined cactus with his boot, "how to create cruel and stubborn life from whatever it is given."

The ground beneath my knees begins to tremble, and then fissure. A clawed hand breaks through the dirt, followed by shoulders and a face that looks like my own, but rendered in spikes and scales and bloodied earth. I see its forked tongue, its snake-fang smile, and then nothing.

Surgery Nightmare
by Caitlyn Palmer

The bright lights burned my eyes, but my eyelids refused to close. The doctor bent down and peered at me. Surely, he could see I was in here…

"Looks like she's out. Alright, put some music on. It's dead quiet in here." I struggled against my body while shuffling sounded behind me. Suddenly, cheerful music started in the room.

"Ah, much better! Now, I'm going to start with an incision here…"

I screamed internally as he sliced into my eye. I thrashed inside my prison and begged him to stop. But he cut again and again, oblivious to my agony.

Burning Love
by Jaimie McGivery

Without a moment's hesitation, Jane poured the remainder of her husband's cologne down the drain, carefully replacing it with a mixture far more potent.

She lay in the dark, waiting. She knew he'd be home late, drenched in her perfume. He'd mask the scent, dousing himself in cologne, before crawling between the sheets, creating a familiar scent she'd come to recognise all too well.

After midnight, she heard the door open, followed by the sound of running water. A wicked smile formed on her face as she heard him scream out, the acid burning deep into his flesh.

Azazel's Heart
by Ann Wycoff

9/1: Today was my third heart operation. I am thankful because the State maintained my Valued Worker status during this difficult time. They removed a non-worker's pacemaker, and after sterilisation, implanted the device in my body.

10/7: Back at work for a week now. Some pain.

10/14: Bad dreams.

10/21: She talks at me even when I'm awake. How? She's dead!

[Subject was clutching a pacemaker, wrapped in paper on which the following text <redacted> had been copied from the banned book, *Azazel's Heart and Other Recipes*. Autopsy concludes subject ripped device from her own chest. Cause of death: Exsanguination.]

Return of the Scimitar
by Clint White

Once his voice was a knife, glassy and serrated, and he'd plunge it through the crunchy guitar ribs of every song. He was the sweaty, shirtless god of the city's basement bars, until the night of the alley fight and the punctured throat. Soon after, the drummer chose hari-kari over the quiet mortal way of fading. Ergo: pact. The singer's blood slivered thinly on parchment before soaking in. The next day he found his old guitarist and shrieked his scimitar tenor right into his face. They booked the last dive on High Street. The drummer returned, too, sullen and incensed.

Green Eyes
by Charlotte Langtree

"Nice eyes."

Tony looked up from stretching his muscles on the bench, surprised to see anyone so early in the morning.

She was a stunner. He smiled, freezing when she moved closer and stroked long-nailed fingers across his cheeks.

"Such a pretty green," she breathed. "May I have them?"

Tony started to pull away, but her grip tightened.

"Look, lady—"

She cut him off by pressing her lips to his. There was a bitterness to her mouth. Tony didn't have the will to protest.

When she took his eyes, he didn't care; the dead have no need to see.

The Demonstration
by Patrick J. Gallagher

"I hope you're paying attention, Williams. This will be on the final exam," said the professor, making the first cut along the top of the forehead. "You see, you don't want to make the incision too deep. Just enough to separate the dermis from the musculature underneath."

The professor gripped the flesh and pulled, tearing the face away, exposing the raw, bloody muscles. Williams, strapped to the bench, his eyes no longer covered by his eyelids, could only stare at his ruined visage in the mirror.

"Now," continued the professor. "Let's see what happens if we cut a little deeper…"

The Zombie Divorce
by Dorn Beaman

I awoke. My head felt heavy, and my vision was blurred into a thousand fractured pieces of darkness.

But I felt no pain.

A vague memory of the monster fluttered at the periphery of my consciousness, and I sought him in gloom.

I saw him eating, but I felt no fear.

The monster's prey looked at me with dead eyes. A hazy memory of those eyes—bright and alive and filled with love for me—floated to the surface but was snuffed out by a white-hot compulsion that blinded my thoughts forever.

I crawled over to share my maker's meal.

Tempest in a Teacup
by Seona Shaw

Staring, outraged, at the 'Do Not Swim' notice, Tempest threw her sable locks over her shoulder.

She glared at the calm water. *Dangerous conditions, my arse!*

She strode, defiant, across the sand and out into the deep.

Tempest swam out too far. When webbed fingers dragged her below, only an unkempt man in a weird hat stood mute witness. Smiling.

No one else heard her thrashing, her screams.

The vodnik held her under. Her final breaths bubbling toward the surface.

A single perfect bubble decanted into a china teacup, the tortured wail of Tempest's soul setting the saucer to rattle.

Come to Me
by L.T. Ward

"I worship you, Death." Her mantra.

Yet Death refused her.

Maven slipped a noose around the neck of the derelict. She'd toppled him running from the crime scene, crimson evidence on his hands.

"Please, no."

Maven wrenched the rope, kicking her boot against his spine, listening for the *snap* before he crumpled.

To the shadow in the dark: "You're here."

The hooded beast raised a bony hand towards her victim.

"Not for you."

"When?"

Death's craggy skull slipped from the cloak, baring a toothless grin. "Soon," it said, fading with its captured soul in tow.

Tomorrow, she would try again.

Almost
by Kara Jones

Marie curled up in the bed, her knees tucked up tight. The duvet was soaked, but she was beyond noticing.

The cold finally broke through her stupor.

Marie sat up carefully, wincing as her lower body unfolded.

Red.

Everything was red—the duvet, her hands, the gouges on her arms, the skin under her nails. Red and sticky, her dress clung to her red-streaked thighs.

Her chest heaved, and she struggled to breathe; her every breath a painful gasp, her throat raw from screaming. Her eyes locked on the swaying mobile with its tiny pastel animals.

She'd come so close.

It's All in Your Head
by S.O. Green

Emily pulled against the leather shackles on her wrists. "What the fuck?"

"Lie still," the surgeon ordered. "Trepanation is a delicate procedure."

"No! Please!"

She struggled. They'd bolted her to the table. She screamed as the whine of the drill seared through her skull, rattled her teeth.

"Stop! Don't let it out!"

Too late. Her crown popped like a champagne cork. Blood fountained. A clawed hand erupted from the hole he'd bored and seized him by the throat. Squeezing. Crushing.

She felt it moving. Cracking bone. Stretching her. Slithering to the floor.

The monster in her head, free at last.

Stuck with Cleanup
by Blen Mesfin

I always had to clean up after them, and it was utterly ridiculous. I contributed to the group just as much as everyone else, but every time we met up, I got stuck with cleaning up at the end.

I'd refused to clean the mess once—it was disastrous. They attempted to cover their own tracks and did a very lousy job of it. The cops had almost caught us with all the evidence they left lying around.

I scrubbed the last stain off the floor and sighed. Removing the blood was easy, getting rid of the body was not.

Suffer the Little Children
by Kennedi Waters

Pain pulses through me like acid blood, searing my veins, pushing it to every cell in my body with each beat of my heart. My eyes fill with red heat, melting irises from the inside. My pinprick pupils make a slow, gory trail down my cheeks.

I scream, but the creature ignores me, an evil grin curls its lips into a snarl as it controls my every thought.

Deep, reverberating words echo in my mind, vibrating through my chest.

The creature throws its plate and startled diners turn to watch, shocked.

My fault; I'd forgotten calamari angers the great Cthulhu.

Donation
by Suann Amero

Gerald rubbed the surface of the bone pendant. He'd done the carving and the abalone inlay. Now, on to the sanding. So very time-consuming, but it really did make the bone shine.

He stilled at the sound of Eva's crutches on the floor; *thump slide thump slide.* As she entered the room, he studied the bandage wrapped around the stump at her knee.

"Almost finished this one," he said, and gave her a pointed look. "Be needing another donation soon."

Tears welled in her eyes. "Can't you find someone else?"

"You've got good bones, baby. No one else will do."

Social Media Bullies
by Furr Kewmal

Don't they know how fucking traumatic this has been? Don't they realise what they're doing to me?

Do they even care?

The lies she spoke—ones my "friends" *blindly* believed. How can they think so little of me? "*Friends.*" Ha! How could I have been so naïve?

I didn't do the things she said. There's proof, but they don't care—"Save your tears, little boy."—too caught up in their schoolyard games for reason.

Hers is the last face I see as I step off the bridge, it follows me into the darkness—she had the last laugh after all.

Rebirth of the Fallen
by Alyson Hasson

A large tree lay on its side, its exposed snaking roots tangling around a young girl. The constricting force pressed into her, rough bark cutting through her delicate skin, streaking her with dark red blood. Her screams echoed across the vast empty field.

The tree sank its roots deep into the dirt, lifting its trunk off the ground and slowly pushing her beneath itself. Tall branches covered in brown leaves shook with pleasure. It had caught a human—it could finally stand again. The crinkled leaves sprung back to life, shining green as the tree stood upright, absorbing her nutrients.

You'll Always Be My Girl
by Dáire Borke

He thrusts and grunts; his weekly treat.

But I only feel the wind teasing my hair, sunshine on my face.

I listen to the trees; malevolent, they whisper his name.

He finishes, pulls up his pants.

"You'll always be my girl," he says, caressing my bone-white cheek, pressing a wet kiss to bloated lips. He pushes my body back into the shallow grave, tenderly re-covers my swollen, black flesh.

He stands when the job is done, leans against the tree. My tree.

Bark separates, he falls inside. Bones splinter and skin rips.

You'll always be my girl, my tree whispers.

My Hands Don't Want Their Skin
by Roxanne Klimek

My hands don't want their skin anymore. They're stripping it away, layer by layer. I wanted them to shine. Scrubbed them, bleached them, to rid the filth. They know I can't. It's ruined.

Skin binds the blood, I told them. My blood is seeping through the cracks. I need to stop washing, convince my hands to heal. I won't stay clean if their skin doesn't protect my blood.

But my blood is already dirty. Rinse it out. Scrub to the bone. My bones will dry. They'll shine. Scrub off the skin, the muscle. To the bone. Down to the bone.

The Dark Trail
by Ken Alders

I scoff at the trail sign which reads: "DEATH AHEAD! TURN BACK NOW!" I adjust my backpack and walk past it without fear.

I never see the pinkish, vile smelling, finger-like tendrils sticking out of the ground until it is too late. I step over the grotesque fingers, and they shoot up, gripping my inner right thigh. I feel my flesh rip, my bone crush, and my blood pour out. The hand begins to pull me down. I scream and black out.

The surreal dungeon in which I find myself has a stranglehold on my soul and commands my doom.

Syn
by Ronnie Scissom

"Her name was Syn, short for Synthetic Replacement Lifeform," Jacob says.

"What was her model number," a female detective asks from across the interrogation room.

Jacob glances down at a tattoo on his wrist made up of three interlocked 6's.

"666," he mutters.

The detective closes her case file and exits the room.

"Sir, he still believes he killed a robot," the detective says to her superior, who's standing at the two-way mirror watching the suspect.

"Patrol found seven more bodies," the weary police chief replies.

"Dear God," she exclaims.

"God doesn't have anything to do with this," he says.

The Husband's Lair
by Nelsim F. Chan

The husband's door was ajar.

His wife entered,
seeking answers
to hushed calls
and midnight retreats.

A travel bag.
Her heart lifted.
Learn Italian.
Couple's Guide to Venice.
Sleeping pills.
His passport.
Eyes closed;
envisioned gondolas,
canal bridges.
grilled octopus tentacles.

Bzzz.

Eyes opened.
Phone vibrations on his desk.
A folder.
She opened it.

Photos.
Eyes widened;
watered.
Mousy neighbour, Trish.
Voluptuous
in a bikini.
Laughing
on the shore,
in the shade
of his shadow.

"Cuppa tea?"

She turned.
He grinned.
Eyes narrowed.
Stared.
She flung
the evidence,
scattering
images.
And a list.
Plastic tarp.
Tape.

The husband's door closed.

Just Out for Some Air
by Dani West

Today I wanted to feel normal again. To do things, I used to enjoy long ago. I slipped out of my home on the hill. Most don't come and visit anymore. Probably because of the overgrowth hiding my world.

Most things have changed in the village, but it's nice to see Appleton Grocer is still around. Suddenly, I was told to leave as I couldn't shop without a mask.

"Why?"

"Because of the pandemic." The annoyed teen pointed to a rising death toll on a magical box. I giggled.

"My simple minded, I assure you I stopped breathing in 1920."

Was it Plato?
by Avery Hunter

Caked in No-Man's-Land mud, ears still ringing from the explosion that took my leg—I haven't yet realised its gone, there's just a dull throb where it used to be—I blink shit from my eyes.

Jimmy lies next to me, a smile on his face. "It's over, Lance," he says, clear as day. "Isn't the end of war beautiful?"

A mortar lands close by. We get showered in dirt again. "What're ya talking about, y'dumbfuck?"

I look over. He's long gone; his brains are seeping into the mud.

"Only the dead have seen the end of war," he whispers.

Calendar Girl
by Mike Murphy

A calendar.

That's what was inside the envelope from her ex. Gwen tacked it up in her bedroom. Pretty pictures. She may as well use it, even though it was from him. Tomorrow *was* the start of a new year.

* * *

She slept fitfully—running fevers, clutching and discarding blankets. The calendar pages flipped back and forth on their own, rushing the seasons outside.

The turning pages became a blur. Gwen's aching bones grated against each other for hours. She awoke seconds before, like kindling, they caught fire.

* * *

Nearby, her ex smiled at his chemistry set when he heard the sirens.

Pitcher Perfect
by Lindsey Harrington

The pitcher of lemonade sweats. Condensation drips and pools on the table. She is unbothered by the heat, but he sweats more than the carafe.

"Do you mind?" he asks, gesturing toward it.

"Go ahead," she answers, smiling.

"Ahhhh, refreshing," he says, blotting his forehead with a napkin.

"Homemade," she explains.

Thirty minutes later, she is dragging his corpse by the ankles. As she hacks the body into chunks, blood drips and pools on the floor. Now, she is sweating.

She blots at her forehead with his napkin, drags her finger through his blood and sucks it off. "Ahhhh, refreshing."

Beyond the Door
by Collin Yeoh

DONT LET HIM IN read the text on my phone. Unknown number.

"Honey! Open the door! It's me!" The voice outside sounded exactly like Carl—but panicked, desperate, terrified.

Another text appeared: *THATS NOT CARL.*

"Honey? Please!" The locked doorknob jiggled in vain, and the frantic pounding shook the door in its frame. "It's coming for me!"

I texted back as fast as I could: *Who r u???*

"Oh God! Oh God, *no!*" Then my husband's voice screamed a blood-curdling scream.

A DISTRACTION ;) came the reply.

I leapt to the door and hurled it open…

But Carl was gone.

Better
by B.A. Nielsen

The two boys stared at him with interest.

"He's a fugly lookin' dude, isn't he?" the older boy said, jabbing a stick deep into his side. "He doesn't even work." The boy gestured at the crow that sat on his shoulder.

"Give him a break," said the younger boy. "He's been here for years."

"Exactly, it's about time we got a new one."

He'd heard enough.

The boys screamed as the scarecrow climbed down from his stand. He grabbed the eldest before he could run away.

"Let's see you do better, you little shit," snarled the Scarecrow, crucifying the boy.

I'm Sorry
by D. Marie Brougher

The punches, the slaps, the hospital stays—you always regretted them later.

"I'm sorry."

The kicks, the spat slurs, the black eyes—always the same words once sober.

"I'm sorry."

The torment, the harassment, your crocodile tears for the lenient judge.

"I'm sorry."

The last cut, the last bruise, the last shovel of dirt on my shallow grave.

"I'm sorry."

My hatred, my anger, my rage—it follows you in your dreams, your waking moments, infests your mind, your consciousness, torments and tortures.

As you press the knife to your pulse and the crimson flows, I whisper…

I'm not sorry.

Mary's Inner Self
by Yvette Appleby

Mary knew the world was full of demons. She saw them everywhere.

Ugliness beneath a thin veil of skin.

Watching her as if she were prey to satisfy their hunger.

She alone could see them.

Maybe I'm the monster, she thought. *The outsider*.

Staring into the mirror intently, she saw it shining—her third eye—buried in her forehead.

She tore at her face and wrenched out the bloodshot orb.

Ripped open her chest, revealing two blue hearts.

Smashed her head against the wall, exposing a yellow brain of snakes.

The remains, when found, were unrecognisable and definitely not human.

Substitute
by Douglas Gwilym

The scrabbling at the screen door isn't her. She's been gone six months. *What do I need a house for?*

Fantasy league's still fun. Beer with the jokers. So why the garbage?

Because it calls to me: an inner tube, a shirt she used to wear. Some inky-pinky clay from the dumpster. Sticks from the park where the trees fuck.

Impossibly, a body comes together under my hands. Sweating in the mirror, I see that its face is my face. I choke.

But when the Subaru starts in the driveway, I pull up the covers. And don't call off work.

Pret a Manger
by Friday Roberts

It's strange, this life we now live—our once prosperous lives have dwindled to this meagre existence.

For instance, I used to get up and jog in the park before breakfast. Shower. Then pop into Pret a Manger for a salted caramel latte and an almond croissant, before catching the train to work and jostling amongst other travel-weary commuters for the whole of my journey.

Now, I don't bother with posh coffee and baked goods—that's a life long past. And there're no jobs to commute to.

But I still run though the park, chasing tasty humans through the trees.

The Familiar
by Clara Brockway

When darkness falls, and the day's echoes falter to silence, I hear my past in the sound of her voice.

I dread the night; it is where she lives, fixed in my memory. I can only see the past through the deep, deep blue of her eyes.

With moonrise, her clever spells cling once more, burning my insides, my guts. And by this, she makes me feel the past.

The subtle poisons used to weaken me fused with my DNA and always bring on exquisite pain.

Now I exist only in the past.

My present and future are all hers.

Storm Cellar
by Marion Lougheed

They told us the southwest corner was the safest spot in the storm cellar, so my sister and I huddled there under the blanket my parents had wrapped around us. Above us, the tornado pounded the steel door like a creature trying to break in. I clutched my sister's arm, and she clutched back.

I was looking up, but I should have been looking down. The whirlwind above my head masked the cracking of the concrete floor beneath my feet.

Cold fingers grabbed my ankle, yanking me down through the hole in the floor. The storm's clamour buried my screams.

The Monster Under the Bed
by Sharron McKenzie

Selina sat on the bed and pulled on a sock. The other sock wasn't on the floor.

She probed the dusty darkness under the bed. As her groping hand found the missing sock, a warm breath blew across her knuckles.

"Sssss…"

Selina put the sock on, then shoved her feet into her shoes.

"SSSelinaaa," whispered the darkness under the bed.

Selina slung her schoolbag over one shoulder.

"Don't go."

Selina frowned. "I can't sit here and dangle my feet for you all day."

"Please…"

Selina shut the door behind her.

The voice grew faint.

"I'm not real when you're gone."

Two Points
by Jim Bates

"Damn," Ellie muttered as Earl's head detached and rolled down the steps like a basketball, coming to rest in a mud puddle. *I shouldn't have cut so deep.*

She continued dragging the headless body of her cheating, drunk of a husband across the front yard into the holding pen where her prize sow, Daisy, was squealing in anticipation.

Ellie grinned and watched as the pig hungerly tore into him and began devouring his dripping intestines.

Then, she grabbed Earl's bloody head and lobbed it in too, watching as it went splat in a pile of manure.

"Two points." She laughed.

Outside the House of the Spiteful Witch
by Samson Stormcrow Hayes

Troy nervously approached the door.

Kelsey teased him. "Are you scared?"

Deanna tried to intervene. "Leave him—"

"Shut it, new girl. You're lucky we asked you along." Turning to Troy. "You want a kiss, go inside."

Deanna muttered, "They say the witch only eats those she hates."

That was enough. Troy turned down the path, running home as fast as he could.

Kelsey looked dejected. She was used to boys doing anything she asked. Then she turned to Deanna, "I bet you're too scared to go inside the witch house."

"I'm not ready to go home."

The witch pounced.

Family
by Jonathan MacDonald

"Mommy? Wake up. Please," he pleaded.

He reached for his mother, wanting a hug, but her lifeless body lay silent and unmoving. Sobbing, he curled into her.

* * *

Later, a loud roar and flash of light stunned him.

"Goddamn it. I hate the fucking kids."

The man looked on in pity at the five-hundred-pound creature that was pushing against the crushed form of what was once a young woman.

He placed his boot on the back of the mewling creature's neck and pushed his blade gently into the base of its skull.

"They don't know their own strength," the man muttered.

All Hare the King
by Buck Charger

The seated jackalope tipped his antlered head to the side.

"Best of the lot?"

"Aye, sire," replied the warren guard.

The black rabbit before him nervously tapped a rear paw.

The jackalope pointed. "Ready to be served— Er, serve your king?"

The rabbit saluted. "Yes, Sire!"

The king leaned back nodding to his guard.

The guard stepped forward, raising his battle axe high.

A squeal escaped the victim, before being cleaved in two.

The king stepped down, regarding the remains. He frowned.

"Ugh, too much tallow," he said, swirling the bloody entrails with a forepaw. "Not worth splitting hares over."

The Mutilation Game
by Andrew Kurtz

As the pinky on her left hand was being slowly severed with a kitchen knife, causing the blood to splatter in her face, Cindy used all her willpower not to scream.

Her right eye was already dangling on a thin membrane after being scooped out with a fork and a rusty razor blade was imbedded in the nipple of her left breast, creating a crimson river of gore.

When her throat was slit with a piece of broken glass, her final thought, as she gazed at her reflection in the mirror, was maybe she'd gone too far with mutilating herself.

The Wild Ones
by Sonya Lawson

"I've always been wild," he drunkenly boasted, following her off the street and into a dark cluster of trees. "But don't be too scared. They say a pretty woman can tame any beast."

She let out an annoyed sigh, turned to block his path, and offered a fake smile with teeth a touch too sharp to be fully human. He froze in fear, and her smile turned genuine. "Please, do tell me more about how beastly you are," she growled.

Later, as she licked his blood off her claws, she wondered why men always thought they were the wild ones.

The Old Ways Are the Best
by Simon Clarke

We all need the food, so I decide a child must die.

Did anyone see him wandering home from school?

I take him home and keep him fresh, out of sight until the moon is right.

I will burn him, bury him in a sacred tumulus.

The seasons turn and it is time. I carry him to the car. Through the ripped black bag, the fresh, frozen boy peers.

I set him alight and send him into another life, where he will ensure the fields will ripen.

Do you see? See the frozen, dead boy's eye following the smoke?

Sycophants
by Rich Rurshell

I watched them drag her from the car, tearing at her clothes. Desperate to prove their loyalty to Satan, they pulled her into a crudely drawn pentagram, pinning her down and forcing her legs apart.

The iron bar was heavy, but wieldy enough to dispatch my oblivious pawns quickly.

I offered my coat and turned my back as she gathered her clothing.

Shaken, but unhurt, the senator's daughter insisted I return with her and meet her father.

He was most grateful for my intervention.

Another senator indebted to us. Our influence knows no bounds. God is dead.

We control everything.

Voices in the Distance
by Grant Butler

John and I were about to head back to camp when we heard voices talking, out in the distance. The voices were hushed and serious. Then in the blink of an eye, the clearing, thick with pine trees, was filled with scattered gunfire, and both of us crouched down to hide.

The air became unnaturally silent. Neither of us dared to move or breathe again until the sole surviving person left. As we walked back to camp, every shadow looked ominous. But when we got there, John said the four most terrifying words I've ever heard: "I dropped my wallet."

The Bay of the Blajini
by Dean Shawker

In line, they trudge to the river's edge, shivering against the Transylvanian spring. Tiny hands hold tight to coloured eggshells in their pockets.

Every year this journey is made—through the cold, dank forests, and down to the Mureş' edge, clutching one another at the merest sound, the quietest snarl.

It's always been this way—*Paştele Blajinilor*—since before I can remember.

I follow the children of the village to the water's edge, careful not to get too close, lest they see my rat's head reflected back, my human formed stripped away.

I've identified the slowest—I'll eat well tonight.

No
by R.M. Hannigan

It's raining at the truck stop. The slick tarmac shines neon light. A sign revolves slowly above the still building. The windows of the truck stop booth are splattered and grimy, but there is no traffic, nor skittering, snuffling animals. He has lain undiscovered here for years, the last sound he heard, a screech of tyres, a scream inside his own skull, the low muttered curse of the little hitchhiker in the short skirt with the inviting thighs.

* * *

It's always raining at the truck stop. He will always be there, undiscovered. He wishes he had listened to her 'no'.

Buffeted
by Kurt Adam

Thistles in the morning mist
Along with steel are moisture kissed
Droplets form, slide to adorn
The sharpened tip of every thorn
And hang there

They watch the clouds that darken slowly
Changing form, grotesque, unholy
Nerve and fortitude are sipped
And rusted courage must be gripped
They wait

The strike is swift, the swords are drawn
Confusion screams and presses on
In leathered arms and armoured feet
Some advance and some retreat
To nowhere

At night, upon the bloodied peat
Lie lumps of shredded gasping meat
Ancient frogs will croak their tune
While the creatures of the moon
Forage

Pentanatos
by Jacek Wilkos

The ritual was almost finished, and four victims were lying on the vertices of the pentagram. I strangled the first with my bare hands, drowned the second, burnt the third on a stake and buried the fourth alive. Their deaths, meant to be a distortion of the five elements, make a mockery of nature and life.

The one I was summoning is their negation, their downfall.

I lay down the last body, the final piece. It's a woman with an open chest, cradling her own heart.

Seeing reality shift, I know I succeeded.

The gate opens for the Unspeakable One.

Sasaeng Fans
by J.F. Garrard

The swarm of sasaeng fans shout praises, declare their love and endless devotion to me, their K-pop idol. The mass of excited schoolgirls surround me, transforming into Hindu gods with countless arms, their sharp nails digging into my eyes, ripping my clothes to shreds and tearing apart my flesh before devouring my soul. My screams of pain cannot override the wave of hormones causing their delirious joy. My red blood, which drenches them, is met with delight as they baste in this unholy baptism. Satisfied with my death, seconds later, they move on to their next prey, their thirst unquenchable.

Wished I'd Stayed Home
by Jonathan Worlde

Tanya struggled to break loose from the giant arachnid's web.

Turned out humans were miniscule on Planet Argonne, relative to the native flora and fauna. Half her crew had been crushed or devoured 48 hours after landing.

Her translator interpreted the anxious discussion between a child alien the size of an Earth house and its mother.

"Don't touch that, honey."

"But, Mom, the cute little bug's going to be eaten!"

"We have to let nature take its course; we can't intervene, no matter how cruel it may seem."

The last thing Tanya saw were immense fangs inside a gaping maw.

Everything But Plastic
by Aaron Lebold

She comes back from the bedroom with the syringe in her hand. She's been prepping there lately. The sickness is the only thing I can think of, and now that I know she has the reprieve, she is my God. She has forgotten about the beatings, the yelling, and the lies— right now she wants to please.

She approaches with a smile and reaches for my arm. She slides the needle in and pushes the plunger. Burning, agonising. Shock and confusion. The tip of the needle is melting, and she smiles wide. "Hydrofluoric acid, melts everything but plastic."

That bitch.

Hungry Restraint
by Quinn Shepherd

Cracks echo through the trees, distracts her from the soft wet kisses he plants across her body.

"Jay? Did you hear that?"

"Mmm?" he replies, mind still on the downward path.

She pulls against soft ropes that bind her to bark. "Someone's here."

He stands, peers into darkness. "I'll go check."

She hears scuffles, cries, then silence.

"Jay?" she calls. Then, as red eyes appear, she screams. "Jay!"

But Jay is already lost; to the thunder in his ears, the red mist, the gnawing hunger.

He drops to his knees, continues the path of red wet kisses on soft flesh.

No Such Thing
by Sherry Osborne

Rain pelted the windows. Lydia shivered in her bed, the blanket wrapped tightly around her shoulders. Lightning turned the room white, but she didn't notice; her eyes were glued to her closet. Scratching sounded from behind the door. She bit her lip to keep from screaming. There was no point. Her parents had already told her there was no such thing as monsters, and she didn't want to make them mad. Thunder rumbled overhead as the closet flew open.

No such thing as monsters, but no one told the creature behind the door. And now it was coming for her.

It Shambles Towards You in the Dark
by C. Dan Castro

"No monster's comin' for you."

Doc says night terrors. Could leave the overhead on, but Billy's almost twelve.

I grasp the light switch. Billy whimpers.

"Look, Billy. I'll guard. In the dark. When you're asleep, I'll go. 'kay?"

Billy gives a curt nod.

"I love you, son."

"Love you, Dad."

Click. Darkness.

"Doin' okay, Billy?

"Billy?

"Billy, answer me. I know you're not asleep. Okay, I'm gonna go..."

But I don't. I flick on the light.

Billy's sheets disarrayed across the bed. Pillow on the floor.

No Billy.

I don't find Billy in his room.
I don't find Billy. Ever.

It Shambles Towards Me in the Dark
by C. Daniela Castro

"No monster's comin' for you." Dad grasps the light switch.

I whimper, knowing *it* is near. Endlessly hunting in its lightless void. Stupid doctor suggested "night terrors."

Dad sighs. "Look, Billy. I'll guard. In the dark. When you're asleep, I'll go. 'kay?"

It's not, but I nod.

"I love you, son."

"Love you, Dad."

Click. Darkness.

"Dad…Dad?"

Squelch.

"Dad!"

Squelch squelch. Closer.

I whip my pillow at the sound. Leap off my bed. Run for Dad. The light switch.

Can't find them.

Backtrack in pitch black, but my bed, room…gone.

Flee into unending darkness, the *squelch squelch* ever nearer.

It Shambles Towards Them in the Dark
by C.D. Castro

Through the door: "No monster's comin' for you."

It's coming for them.

Billy answers his father by whimpering, undoubtedly sensing *it* beyond the void's barrier.

I whisper forgotten words.

The barrier thins.

Just needs darkness.

Murmuring... "Love you, Dad."

Billy's sweet, but that's not why he's here.

Click. Dad killing the lights.

Billy's here because he'd have power.

"Dad?"

And he does. Vast. Unharnessed.

Squelch.

It stirs, clawed tentacles perfect for shearing flesh. For cracking bones to slurp marrow.

It'll devour Billy. And his power, some escaping.

To me.

Billy's a sweet boy.

But I can always have another child.

I Shamble Towards You in the Dark
by C. Danny Castro

Through the barrier, a boy's whimper.

His mother whispers, forgotten words. The barrier thins...

I hear her desire. If I devour her progeny, Billy, some power will slip by. To her.

The barrier vanishes.

But Billy's young. He'll grow succulent.

Billy stumbles into the lightless void. My tentacles reach out. The mother leans in to catch any scintilla I miss.

My tentacles ensnare her arms and legs before she realises. One tentacle worms down her throat, silencing further forgotten words.

Billy flees into the darkness.

As I suck down morsels of the mother, I dream of the day Billy ripens.

Show Time
by Amber M. Simpson

"There are no clowns hiding in the dark," Aly's mommy says, turning out the light. "I promise you'll be fine. Sweet dreams, honey."

Parents are always making promises they can't keep.

In the dark, Aly sniffles, clutching tight her fuzzy bunny.

It's show time.

I slide out from beneath the bed, back stiff from lying in wait. My bells jingle as I get to my feet, goofy grin stretching my painted face. Honking my big red nose with one white-gloved hand, I giggle and raise my knife with the other.

Their screams are the best part of all my routines.

Mrs Carol
by Mendel Mire

My doll of you is the best toy ever.

When you gave me that detention, it was fun to twist my doll's leg backwards. You needed to have hip surgery afterwards and couldn't teach us for months.

When you sent me to the principal's office, it was fun to push pins through my doll's eyes. You've needed those dumb coke-bottle glasses ever since.

This time, you've given me an F for my exam. And now Mum and Dad won't buy me the tablet they promised.

Now I'm keen to see what happens when I drop my doll into the blender.

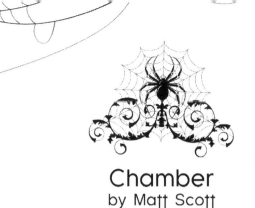

Chamber
by Matt Scott

I've been made aware—rather auspiciously, I might add—that some find what I do for a living offensive, immoral even. I want to assure those in attendance tonight at this meeting (hosted by the very lovely Mrs Verily Ashworth, and held in this magnificent hall) that while my occupation may be to some unsettling, I can tell you with confidence and certainty, that it must be done for the good of the aggregate. Now, if you would be so kind as to disrobe and link hands with the person next to you, this will all be over very soon.

Diabolus
by Denver Grenell

The church band staggered to the end of a painfully slow rendition of "O Come All Ye Faithful."

With a dark smile, Duayne, the guitarist, turned his amplifier up until it squealed with feedback, then played the Devil's tritone—the *diabolus in musica*. The sinister notes caused the stunned congregation to clasp hands over their ears, but to no avail.

Reverend Cartwright was the first to start bleeding from the eyes, his screams melding with the cacophony. The shrieks multiplied into a choir of the damned and the floor of the cathedral soon swam with a thick river of blood.

Tooth Fairy's Revenge
by Nancy Rule

She's always careful when doing a new pickup. This guy set a mousetrap with a yellowed tooth as bait. He snores loudly while waiting.

She texts for back up. Flying countless times around his head, arms, and body, she uses tooth floss to lash him to his chair.

A hundred fairies bombard in. They land as he opens his eyes. He screams, brushing them off, and she sinks her fangs into his fat cheek. The poison works immediately to immobilise him.

"Who's hungry?" They grin, baring rows of sharp teeth. Human flesh will be a delicious change from baby teeth.

Venom of God
by Elizabeth Nettleton

"His mum died," Meredith whispered through the phone.

"Oh, bless him! I'm glad he has you now."

Meredith smiled as small fingers wrapped around her thumb. Cradling the baby to her chest, she ran through the names she'd always wanted to use.

Samael, she decided. *My son.*

Pain seared through her breast. Meredith screamed and pulled away, her shirt now stained red. Samael's eyes blackened above his grin, and blood dribbled through his gaping teeth. He spat out a chunk of flesh and launched forward, tearing into Meredith's throat.

My son, she thought as she took her last breath. *Mine.*

All the Headlights Shining
by Emma Phillips

We all called him Mr Hal, although the rest of us were just our badge names: Ruby, Sam, Diego. He never spoke much but polished the counter till the truckers dined off their reflections. He'd fire you if you were late.

We knew the rumours; he still set a place for her out back, made up her bed, bought a fancy cake and added pink candles each year for her birthday. They never found a body. She was last seen out front. Mr Hal raised the alarm when he found her bike toppled in the lot, its wheels still spinning.

Among the Weeds, Across the Pond
by R. Wayne Gray

Todd floated to a stop. That wasn't a tire, but the bloated, blackened flesh of a waterlogged corpse near the shore.

Todd backpaddled.

Bobbing lightly, the corpse followed. Todd spun the kayak around and raced for the distant pier.

Halfway across. The corpse was gaining. The face cleared water, a dull, milky eye, glaring.

Paddles blurred. Something bumped the kayak. Todd screamed, and families fishing on the pier gathered.

Kayak met wood, and Todd whipped around. The corpse…was floating placidly, thirty yards out.

"What's that, Mister?" someone asked.

Todd let out a breath. "Someone who wanted to be found."

This Means War
by Wednesday Paige

I can't remember a time when it wasn't like this—the *why* has evaporated into ancient history.

"Cheeky fuckers!" Rick had exclaimed after receiving their note: "You were loud last night. 'I'm coming!' 3 times (yeah, right)."

I thought he'd be satisfied with knocking copper nails into their precious trees…until one fell onto our garage.

They're not so innocent either: sneaking into our garden to steal our chickens; taking our post; filling our dustbin after it's been emptied.

I can't help thinking it's gone too far as he pulls their bulging-eyed chihuahua—its tongue hanging out—from our freezer.

Liver Spaghetti Sauce
by Joshua E. Borgmann

Retrieve a liver. It must be selected carefully. A liver from a virgin female in her twenties is best, but hard to come by. High end escorts are excellent alternatives. Avoid livers from aged alcoholics, as disease ruins taste.

Grind the liver.

Add a little fat from the stomach or thighs during the grinding process.

Pour extra virgin olive oil in a skillet and sauté onions and garlic. Add the liver to it.

Cook until brown.

Add one can of diced tomatoes. Stir.

Season to your taste.

Reduce heat and simmer for twenty-five minutes.

Serve with pasta of your choice.

Party Boat
by Alexandra Haverská

The heat was on in Normandy. A party boat anchored in the old basin of Le Havre pulsated. Drinks, laughter, the below-decks rumbling in concert. People danced to summer and life. And their cries and stomping awakened the depths.

A figure materialised in the corner: a pallid sailor, still damp from the ascent.

"Hello, pretty, a lil' dance?"

Le Havre de Grâce, the Haven of Grace. Perchance he'd find some graces tonight. The lust and vigour pouring from the partying people resonated in the deep below.

More and more dead came out of the water, mingling freely with the living.

Fresh Meat
by Wondra Vanian

Nigel ran. The woods weren't his first choice of escape, but the police were closing in.

"Agh!"

He clamped a hand across his mouth to muffle the scream as he fell. Reaching down, he felt steel.

A bear trap?

"Well, look at you…"

Relief flooded Nigel. Not a cop, just some yokel. He'd have to kill her too, after she freed him.

"We've had worse." A man joined them, axe in hand.

She sighed. "I was hoping for something with a bit more meat on 'im."

"He'll do."

Not a *bear* trap, Nigel realised, when the man raised his axe.

A Consequence of Calling
by Colin Leonard

"Nice house," he said. "Very contemporary."

She wept in the corner.

"Usually, I end up in old ruins…forests…that kind of thing. And you're not wearing a robe. They usually wear robes, if they wear anything at all."

He picked between his teeth with a sharp, black fingernail, stepping over the clump of bodies at his feet.

"Were they related to you? You've got the same nose as that one there. Well, when he had a nose."

"You ate their faces," she wailed.

"Well, you're the one who summoned me. What did you think I was going to do?"

Prince of Hell
by Jennifer Canaveral

Valak had a mission: murder Sarah, retrieve her soul. With Sarah cowering in the basement, the Devil's cherubic prince had his prey cornered, the nights of playing cat-and-mouse gone. Valak would eliminate Sarah, only not as the spectre from her nightmares but as a mortal. As equals.

Sarah stared into Valak's obsidian eyes, his tiny hands cradling her chin. Repulsed, she reached out and grabbed his throat. Sarah sunk her nails into his gaunt neck, then squeezed, squeezed, squeezed until she punctured his carotid arteries.

Valak collapsed.

Blood gushed across the floor as an impish smile spread across Sarah's face.

Dreamland
by Renee Schnebelin

Emma reached out towards the shadowy figure that was just floating above her bed. He didn't move, he didn't speak.

Was he actually real?

She knew that the Shadow Man wasn't real, but at times it felt as if he could dip into her very soul and steal it if he were to ever reach her while she was asleep.

Dreamland was beginning to blend in with reality, creating a chaotically braided world filled with dark alleys, floating red orbs, and sometimes the Shadow Man—with his top hat always perfectly placed and a presence that filled Emma with terror.

Escape from the House in the Woods
by Simon J. Plant

From the woods, I emerge and see a *diner!* Only the road's too quiet; the diner's abandoned. Hungry. Running. Scared. Vile torture. My narrow escape was all for nothing.

But salvation is an approaching car!

Terrorised, raped, I climb in with bloodied clothes. "Drive," I tell my Samaritan. "Don't stop."

"Where?"

"Hospital. Police—"

Rough hands grip the wheel.

Captive for seven days, shackled in the basement—I never saw a face. He was always masked. But his hands were workingman's; nails packed with grime…

I notice there's no handle on the passenger door. No way out.

The Samaritan grins.

Lost in the Dark
by Gary Clifton

Daddy's ancient pickup sputtered as Marilou coasted into a closed station. Home, only a mile down the lane, she started the cold, rainy trek.

Headlights, then a man's voice. "Need a lift?"

Hesitant. "O-okay."

Shortly; "Okay, babe, lose them wet duds."

"Oh God, no, mister. I got a bad ailment. It's fatal. Please don't."

He ripped at her soggy dress.

"God, make it stop!" she sobbed.

* * *

"Sheriff," the trooper leaned down. "He's torn to shreds. Throats gone…like, eaten?"

"Sure looks possible. We had a similar incident two months back. Hillbillies hereabouts claim a werewolf prowls these woods. Dumb hayseeds."

379

The Cure
by Khana W. Reeds

"I love you," she'd said with eyes so sad, I wanted to take her in my arms.

"But it can't be," I'd replied, though it burned my heart. "We're so different, you and I."

She'd scowled then, the action wrinkling her nose into cuteness.

"What if I promise not to share special kisses with you?" she'd offered with a sniff.

I wanted so badly for her to share my life. But the sacrifice was huge. Especially for her.

She gazed up at me, smiling lovingly, from beneath watery lashes as I finished the stitch that would seal her lips forever.

A Death Anniversary
by Armand Gloriosa

When I was a kid, my driver told me a story.

Early one morning, a senior high school girl waited beside this very road for a friend's car. She got into the wrong one by mistake and was later found raped and murdered. Afterwards, her ghost could be seen every year, at the time and day of her death. He'd seen her once or twice for himself.

"Oh, really? A high school girl like that one right there? Let's pick her up."

"No. Please don't."

"Here she comes. Wait— Her uniform is decades out of date."

"Drive. Drive, damn it!"

Growing Pains
by Gloria Martin

Jacob always felt intense pleasure as he ate. An exquisite pain flowing through his growing bones. He didn't remember his father. Mother said he provided for him for a while.

One day, Mother said she was leaving, but would provide for him like his father.

The next day, when Jacob squeezed into the house from his barn, his mother lay on the floor. He knew what to do. Consuming her was like nothing he felt before. His body grew even larger.

He looked forward to the coming night and fending for himself amongst the isolated villages in the next valley.

When Love Leaves
by Matt Brinkerton

Love will not endure just by loving. It died on your lips, and I knew all hope was lost of my heart ever mending.

From then, my dreams became twisted. The exquisite pain was overwhelming, and eventually a dark, lonely rapture had its way.

I studied the old texts and prepared my prayer for All Hallows' Eve.

* * *

The time is here. "Em egneva ot su tsgnoma emoc efil dna thgil fo drol ythgiM."

I turn away as Asmodeus coalesces from the crimson cloud and leaves to destroy my love.

* * *

Grey truth, glowering over each day, transformed my love into hate.

Roxanne
by Beckett Van Stralen

My sister died recently. I've been dealing with her belongings. After her death, I found a sticky note that seemed hidden away behind her computer. Scrawled was a website URL.

I decide to thumb the address into her internet browser. The URL is a file directory. Everything listed is saved under a first name. I find the most recent file—a video titled *Roxanne*.

I see my sister's lifeless body suspended in front of her computer like a marionette. Something manipulates her limbs in false animation. The webcam flashes. It's over.

I move to stand but can't.

The webcam flashes.

Rejection
by L.J. McLeod

"Unfortunately…" the email began. She didn't bother reading the rest. These rejection emails were all the same. This one stung though. A lot of research and hard work had gone into this story. Why wouldn't they publish it? She walked over to the chest freezer and opened the lid. It was filled with neatly dissected body parts that she had carefully wrapped and stored. What had she got wrong? Clearly, more research was needed. She grabbed her phone and ordered another pizza for delivery. This time she would get the details right and they would have to publish her story.

Partners Under the Moon
by Nikki R. Leigh

I heard her close behind me, the soft crunching of leaves under feet. The screen door rattled as she pawed at the metal grate. The black dog had followed me home.

Kneeling to face her through the screen, I smelled stale blood on her teeth. I told her to wait just a little while longer, so she curled up into herself on my porch, doing just that.

She heard me yowl from inside my home. Shedding my skin, breaking bones. Her ears perked up as she remembered last month's hunt. She was eager to do it again.

So was I.

Tradition
by R.A. Goli

Her skin split like taut cling wrap cut with a sharp fingernail. He smiled as blood gushed out, throbbing with each pump of her heart. She screamed through her gag.

He stretched the wound open with his hands, then sawed away chunks of muscle and connective tissue, until he had a clear view of the bone.

He washed away some blood—it was pumping out much slower now—then picked up his scribe and started carving his design.

Both his father and grandfather were scrimshanders, but it was illegal to use whale bone now. So, he had to make do.

Scurry
by Raven Isobel Plum

They scavenge, scurry, rub sharpened claws together in scheming anticipation. Parasitic, driven by an ever-aching hunger. Entering houses once occupants are still—destroying everything dear with fire or ferocity. The woods are their realm. Preternatural strength. Most think they simply bury nuts, but not once they have a taste for flesh.

Liam made that mistake. He'd watch at dawn, adoring their camouflage of cuteness. Tossing them peanuts, watching their acrobatics. Liam fell asleep with his hand in the paper peanut bag. His screams echoed through the park when he awoke to hideous nubs of fingers that used to be.

Subdermal
by Isaac Menuza

There's a woman under my skin.

They dared me to spend a night in the hollow, and now there's a woman under my skin.

A sleepless eve in that cavernous tree, listening to the foxes scream. Still, she took me.

Our bones grind, every movement full of shrapnel. My flesh bulges, splitting at pink seams that ooze translucent discharge. Yellow nails pierce my fingertips, spear-like finials guiding her restless digits to light.

I'll cut her out.

The knife's point seeks the welt in my neck: her nose clogging my throat.

Before I jab, she exhales through my mouth, "*Do it.*"

Homogeneity
by Olivia Ava

My mind is tired, my body too. My past is bleak, full of storm clouds, full of death, full of despair. I can see nothing different in my future; just a slow, aching trudge to the end. Counting down days, and hours, and minutes in wretched repose until the inevitable, ultimate climax.

The psychiatrists give me little white pills. "You'll soon feel better," they say.

I don't. I don't feel anything.

No depression, no fugue, but no joy, no love, no happiness either. Just homogeneity.

I swallow down the last pill, lie back, and close my eyes one last time.

Food Photography Advice
by K. Wreeds

I have a photograph of every meal I've eaten since I came to this house with its high fences and fancy darkroom. It's not like the old days when I could use my phone's camera—the electricity is long dead. I've learnt to use a Nikon FM2 with 35mm film—lining up the shot, getting the lighting right, the angle just so. It's a great camera.

* * *

The zombie—not known for stealth—clumsily shambles through the trees, stalking some kid. I set up the shot.

And shoot.

The kid falls.

The Remington takes a much better shot than the Nikon.

Nine Lives
by K.B. Elijah

I claw at the edge of the wound, fingertips scrabbling for the loose skin, which is now bloody and slick, and *pull*.

Flesh slowly peels away from the glistening mess beneath as my arms strain with the effort of heaving the taut drape of skin from my body. My hoarse screams drown out the wet squelch of my bare—not just shoeless, but *soleless*—feet slapping onto the tiles as I step out of my birthday suit.

My first life. Carelessly lost in a drunken bar fight.

But I still have eight lives left, my new skin shiny and pink.

Terms of Service
by Jade Wildy

"If I can't have your heart, no one can."

His fingers dug into her neck. His breath, stale as death.

She shook and clutched a hand to her chest. Her heart thudded. She pressed further, digging nails into her flesh, forming bloody crescents. Harder she pushed, her ribs stretching then snapping with little crack sounds. Deeper her fist sank, past her breath-filled lungs, droplets of blood dribbling down her palm, until her hand clenched around it.

She held her heart out to him, still beating with remembered rhythm.

"If that's your terms, then take it. I'd rather be without it."

Seeking Asylum
by Mariya West

The woman's watery laughter floats through the room of clouds. She reminisces.

* * *

The drunk dug greedy fingers into her panties. "You stay until I get fucked."

A scream. His.

A glint of metal penetrated his thigh.

In Clint Eastwood hoarseness, she whispered, "Well, Punk, now you're fucked."

* * *

Her motorcycle revved along the island; swerved.

A turtle.

The truck behind didn't.

It overtook her.

She followed patiently.

Her bloody sheath dripped in its ankle holster.

* * *

A metal door booms open.

She rubs her nose on the soft wall.

Blurred angels unlace straps.

A gleam of silver pricks then pierces her skin.

Practice Limitations
by Mari Ness

He was getting better at this. He knew that. His stitches were neater, finer, faster. When necessary—a phone call, a meal, a knock on the door—he could even set one or two stitches one handed, without looking directly at them. He had even begun to experiment. Different colours, different thicknesses, different materials. Though that was partly by necessity; he kept running out of nylon thread. And yet, no matter how skilled he became, he could not stop the blood from soaking into the thread or sew fast enough to keep his skin attached to his muscles and bones.

The Acolyte
by Karen Bayly

"Invite me in!"

I obeyed, plunging a hunting knife into my gut, slashing my belly open from groin to breastbone. My intestines gushed onto the floor, but I continued to butcher my torso, screaming as I ripped out my liver, stomach, and sex organs. Blood streaming down my arm, I held my uterus aloft and ululated.

The acolyte gurgled and slithered inside. Its tail fastened into my vagina. Its body coiled in my abdominal cavity, head pushing upwards until it abutted against my larynx. Then it zipped me up like a flesh onesie.

I was ready to serve our master.

Pick a Game from the Compenium
by Keely O'Shaughnessy

There's something odd about our town. Clouds hang lower. Nights are darker.

I pass the daylight hours with my sister. Cluedo is out, as is the tig part of tag, and her translucence provides unfair advantage in hide-and-seek, so I turn out cards for solitaire.

The deck—initials inscribed on the lid—is our father's. Sometimes she traces the ornate script, fingertips hovering. And sometimes, as dusk approaches, the slit at her throat becomes an opening, lacerated tissue, blood seeping, staining the one-eyed Jacks.

As I said, there's something odd about our town, the dead don't always stay that way.

Shadow
by Cassandra Angler

Ellen had just seated herself at the table with a full plate when the doorbell rang. She peered through the peephole on the door, seeing no more than the top of a dark-haired head. Ellen sighed and opened the door. A little girl stared up at her with eyes as black as coal, her thin lips grinning.

"Can…can I help you?" Ellen stammered, unnerved.

The child motioned her closer, and Ellen leaned forwards. With a giggle, the child's jaw unhinged to twice its size, slamming shut around Ellen's head.

Ellen's body dropped, and the child left with a belch.

Mr Gangly
by Jay Baird

Sounds coming from the attic again.

Thump. Thump.

Lucy hugs her stuffed bear and looks at the ceiling.

Thump. Thump.

The thing in the attack is moving again. It's looking for something to eat. *It's looking for me*, she thinks.

Scraping sounds now. The sound of the attic entrance being pulled aside. Lucy pulls the blanket over her head. She lies as still as she can.

Thump. Thump.

The sound of footsteps on the landing.

Lucy risks a look at her door. A wizened, gaunt hand with elongated fingers is wrapped around the frame. It begins to move.

Thump. Thump.

My Money's No Good There
by Susan Vita

It's midnight. The "fill tank" light is blinking, and I'm famished.

At last, I see an open gas station.

"Pay inside," a voice commands.

Inside, the store smells like stale Camels.

"What brings you out on a night like tonight?" asks the cashier, leering at my leather miniskirt.

"Just gas, please."

Someone from behind me tries to pin me against the counter. The cashier smiles at me.

A greasy hand paws at my skirt, and I smile back.

He freezes, and I trap Mr. Grabby-Hand's arm, ripping it off at the shoulder before sinking my teeth into his warm flesh.

A Ghost Story
by S.A. O'Driscoll

We watch for you.

As you walk past store fronts, can't you see us standing behind you? Our clothes are spotted with mould, our skin is mottled with rot. Our lips are sewn shut, as are our eyes.

It's just as well that you can't see us because you will never know how close you come to being strangled by our dirt-caked hands. You are oblivious to the fact that we would love nothing more than to drag you six feet down so our bones can strangle you. It's your turn to be the feast for the worms and maggots.

Give me a name
by Renee Cronley

The case has gone cold. They tell me there are no trails that lead to finding her murderer. They said she was an addict—an architect of her own choices until her last breath. So I choose to tear the world apart to find out his name until mine. The moon shines a path along the earth my sister was returned to. She once faded in and out of my life, but her tombstone rises out of the dirt with a certain degree of permanence. My eyes rest on her name until she whispers mine. Then I ask for his.

Amfi Bee Ann
by David Green

There was a frog, up in a tree

I sat below. A deep croak, "Hello!"

It made me jump; thought I was alone

I did not know, it was his home

Green slime he dripped, upon my head

Too tired was I, 'twas time for bed.

I closed my eyes as dark went skies

The slime did sink into my skin

When I awoke, green slime had soaked

Into my brain. My God, the pain!

Verdant hues my skin did go

Irk did throw my right hook

Frog left the branch—a graceless plunge

That evil frog, I did expunge.

They Land
by Sierra Silver

This plague that stole her voice will decimate the planet's population. Silent anguish vibrates through her. Tears fall, clouding her premonitions.

The invasion will start so benignly. Just a handful of them at a time. They'll seem friendly, helpful. A show of faith. Offerings of agricultural technologies, processes. Enhanced medical technology—physiology too different for their medicines.

That alone will stymie them, slow them. But not stop them. They'll turn to the food, the water. Slower but just as effective.

Blinking, back in the present, she watches the human's ship land.

Her visions had lied.

They'd poisoned the water first.

The Limitless Regret
by Suzanne Baginskie

Sheila followed Cousin James and his mates through an abandoned factory window, disregarding tomboy warnings from her mum.

Instead of partying, evil creatures hidden in shadows stormed James and chomped away. Horrified, the guys scrambled toward an exit, knocking Shcila facedown. She landed on rotted floorboards, covered in blood oozing from partially devoured humans.

Above her, zombies circled James' screaming pals and feasted on their brains. Flesh flew, bones cracked, before they trudged her way.

With no chance of escape, slimy hands seized her trembling body, their last tempting meal.

Sheila uttered, "Damn, if only I'd listened to my mum."

Home Invasion
by Annya Alexander

Ragno twitched nervously when she felt the first vibration. The tremor juddered through her home, knocking one of her babies to the floor.

She ignored the pleading eyes as it reached up to her, and scuttled to the very edge of her property, the hair on her body thrumming with each tremble.

"*Them...*" she whispered, hearing the invaders' voices.

Her babies, much practiced, scrambled over each other to get into their positions in the huddle.

Then a pregnant pause as they waited for *them*.

"Fuck-fuck! Robert!" The female human screamed as a thousand spiderlings dropped onto her head at once.

It Goes to Bed with Me
by Michael Anthony Dioguardi

I stay up all night.

I scream when it comes for me. My brother peeks over the bunk bed rail. He's amused, but I can tell he's also terrified. I can hear Mom and Dad's footsteps in the hall.

"He's too old for this," Mom says.

"Well, the doctor said they could go on for longer," Dad replies.

My eyes are wide open, but I cannot see.

"Peter, honey. Come on now…" she pleads.

I'm being smothered.

"I…I…" I struggle to whisper.

It crawls out from under my skin. It replaces me.

It is me.

"I'm not Peter," it croaks.

Blocked
by L.T. Emery

My head is shackled in place, my mouth clamped open. I sit in my own waste. The straps are pulled so tight I've lost all feeling in my hands and feet.

I've no idea how I got here—wherever here is—it's pitch-black. I'm terrified beyond belief.

Light flares from above and a body silhouettes my view. He's huge. I'm in a basement. The steps groan as he descends.

"Hello @gamerexpert," he growls. "Remember me? I'm @kingdaddy. You blocked me. Stole my voice. Now, I'll take yours."

The cold pliers lock onto my tongue, and I scream one last time.

Clown Mask
by John Kujawski

Perhaps she had a message for me when I walked into the booth. It was one of those adult acts I was interested in. The curtain rose, and she appeared through the glass. It wasn't a beautiful face I saw, but a woman in a horrific clown mask. She stared at me angrily—I could see it in her eyes.

I later became obsessed with the image of the woman. She'd brought something out in me.

One night, I had a date and brought a package. I couldn't wait to give my girlfriend the mask I wanted her to wear.

The Shadow in the Mirror
by Rotten Akers

Being strangled by unseen hands wasn't my idea of a nice vacation, but I guess it was when I decided to stay at that haunted hotel.

You could only see it in the mirrors. Even now, I check them to be sure it's not there glaring at me with its hollow eyes.

I don't know what I did to upset it. The reason I'm writing this is that I saw it through my bathroom mirror, standing behind me in the shower.

I've been awake for hours, and I can't keep my eyes open much longer. I hope I don't die.

Survival
by Chisto Healy

Tara was shivering—blood loss was taking its toll. She swung back and forth, hanging upside down from the rafters in the barn. If she wanted to have any hope of making it out alive, she had to fight exhaustion and get herself down.

Tara knew the man in the pig mask that was soaked in the blood of her friends would return for her before long. She had to get free of the ties that bound her to the beam. With nothing but her teeth to use, she bent upwards and worked to chew through her own exposed intestines.

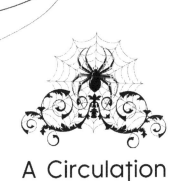

A Circulation
by Megan Feehley

There is beauty just before the terror. The silken breath taken before the spill of righteousness. The warmth of a licking flame preceding the scald. The love that twists and writhes underneath my skin; leaving wormy pathways I feel against the reverence of your fingers.

We are electric. Embrace the current racing from the ground and up your legs. It's all connected, tangled up, woven together in a mass of threads. A thousand eyes rip into us. I like the way the smoke and ashes fill your vision with black tears.

Death looks so incredibly alive in your eyes.

Acknowledgements

When we embarked on our Black Hare Press journey back in late 2018, we never envisioned the huge support we'd get from the writing community. We've been truly humbled by the number of submissions received and have loved reading every single one.

To the talented authors who crafted tales just for us—from drabbles, all the way through to novels—we thank you from the bottom of our hearts.

To our families and friends, collaborators, random strangers who took pity on us, and all who helped us on the way: we couldn't have done it without you.

Special thanks to our Patreon supporters, especially S. Jade Path, James Aitchison and Jonathan Stiffy. Take a look at the Patreon-only content and merch here— patreon.com/blackharepress—and consider helping us get to the next stage.

And to you, our discerning reader, we and these talented writers did it all for you. We hope you enjoyed the tales, and if you did, don't forget to leave a review.

Thank you all—see you next time.

Love & kisses
The Black Hare Press Team

About the Publisher

BLACK HARE PRESS is a small, independent publisher based in Melbourne, Australia.

Founded in 2018, our aim has always been to champion emerging authors from all around the globe and offer opportunities for them to participate in speculative fiction and horror short story anthologies.

Connect: linktr.ee/blackharepress

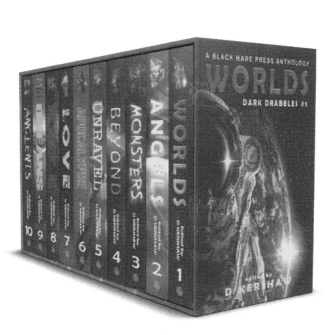

439

Printed in Great Britain
by Amazon